Musical

Youth

By Joanne C. Hillhouse

Cover Illustration by Glenroy Aaron

Joanne C. Hillhouse is the Antiguan and Barbudan author of The Boy from Willow Bend, Dancing Nude in the Moonlight, Fish Outta Water, and Oh Gad! Her fiction, non-fiction and poetry have been published in various international journals and anthologies. Joanne lives in Antigua and from there she freelances across borders as a writer, editor, and writing coach; and runs the Wadadli Youth Pen Prize writing programme to nurture and showcase the literary arts.
Read more about Joanne's work at wadadlipen.wordpress.com and jhohadli.wordpress.com

Musical Youth is the 2014 second place winner of the inaugural Burt Award for Young Adult Caribbean Literature.

Text copyright @2013 Joanne C. Hillhouse
Cover Illustration copyright @2014 Glenroy Aaron
All rights reserved.

CaribbeanReads Publishing, Basseterre, St. Kitts, West Indies
Second Edition

ISBN: 978-1-7338299-5-3 Paperback Second Edition (2019)
978-1-7338299-6-0 Hardcover Second Edition (2019)
978-0-9899305-1-2 Paperback First Edition (2014)
978-0-9899305-1-2 Paperback
978-0-9899305-4-3 Ebook
Library of Congress Control Number: 2014952394

Printed in the USA

Acknowledgements

I feel blessed that this book is going in to its second printing. I give thanks to God for that and to family and friends who have supported me in any way.

Thanks also to Caribbean Reads for continuing to believe in Musical Youth; and to CODE, the Burt Award, and the Bocas Lit Fest for berthing this story into the marketplace.

I give thanks for the people and stories that inspired Musical Youth, and to all the creators of music who inspire me.

Thanks to readers everywhere—*tout monde sam and baggai*, as we say in Antigua and Barbuda—who bought and/or took the time to recommend the book; and specifically, Caribbean readers and young people who have told me how much they love Zahara, and how Zahara and Shaka are #relationshipgoals.

To reviewers and bloggers (the late Hazel Campbell among others); to anyone who shared their platform (authors, media, etc.); to book stores (especially local bookstore Best of Books which has hosted all my launches to date); to book clubs and lit fests that invited me; to the schools that welcomed me in Antigua and elsewhere; to the schools that have added it to their reading lists(with hopefully more to come), thank you; to every and anyone who continues to give this book life.

I have to shout out Ashley Bryan whose story, "The Dancing Granny," the kids in the book are staging as their summer production. As his story inspired me, I hope the characters in my story inspire young people to find their passion and live their purpose.

I dedicate this second edition of Musical Youth to the memory of Alstyne Allen, the person I called at three in the morning when I read that I was a finalist for the Burt Award. She saw the struggles, but never doubted the journey, and always encouraged me to celebrate even the little triumphs. Alstyne, who died suddenly in 2015, was my sister-friend in the truest sense.

#thepowerofpositivethinking

Chapter 1

Zahara, like the Sahara.

That's the rhyme her mom used to sing to her when she was little to help her remember her name and to teach her how to spell it. It was her earliest memory. Even now, the echo of her mother's voice singing the made-up tune was her bedtime lullaby, though it grew fainter with each passing year.

Everything about her was like an echo of her mother, not quite as vivid as the original. There were her eyes, brown like a rusty penny. There was her dimple, a left cheek dimple, none in the fat right cheek. There was her butternut-coloured skin and her thick, bushy, Brillo Pad-textured hair. She had vague memories of sitting between her mother's knees to get her hair combed, her mother tugging and pulling, trying to tame the untameable while she winced and cried. When she looked in the mirror it was her mother—and yet not quite her mother—who stared back, like a bad artist's impression, or a faded watermark.

Sometimes she felt the disappointment of that in the way her grandmother looked at her. Granny Linda had raised her since the car accident that had killed her mother, the accident that had happened when she was still too little to understand what the loss of a mother meant, much less the loss of a daughter.

Granny Linda didn't say, "I wish she was here instead of you." She probably didn't even think or feel it; but it always sort of felt like she might, like, who would want a copy when the real thing was always better.

"Girl, you crisp like new money."

That's how he stepped to her.

She didn't even spare him a glance, and it wasn't just Granny Linda's warnings about boys and their not-so-good intentions. It wasn't even that she thought he wasn't good enough for her though he was a sort of rough looking youth. But she had her guitar over her shoulder, and, as much as she loved music, she was always self-conscious on the days she had to lug the bulky instrument with her for after school choir practice. It was a way to draw attention to oneself, and she was so used to blending in, she tended to prefer it.

He didn't get the memo though, trailing behind her as she trailed behind the flock, as always; the sidewalk ahead of them a crowd of plaid jumpers mixed in with purple ones from the school further up the road, the boys in white shirts and khaki pants.

She didn't know his name, he didn't know hers, and wouldn't if she had anything to say about it, with his forwardness, jumping right in and chatting her up like they were long-time friends. He didn't seem to mind her silence, picking up both sides of the conversation when she didn't answer right away.

"So, you play guitar."

"Yeah, me like music too, nuh."

"Yeah…"

"Me like hip-hop mostly."

"Yeah…"

"Yeah, me like Bob Marley though, he min wicked pon the guitar, right?"

She almost answered then. Bob Marley's "Redemption Song" was the first thing she'd learned to play on her own, no hand guiding hers, no chords to

3

follow; the first song she'd taught herself, playing along with it on the radio, fiddling with it from memory. When she'd mastered it, she'd felt so proud of herself she'd almost auditioned for the school pageant, the winner of which got to represent first her class in the school's Talented Teen-Best of Forms then, if victorious, her school in the Teen Splash at Carnival.

That had been a year ago. She'd been in first form, still new to secondary school and too shy to raise her hand. She'd stayed after school for the auditions, with the other hopefuls and their hecklers. She'd sat in the back, the red and black Stella Harmony propped up next to her too conspicuous for her to really hide. Others flaunted their talents. It was like a party. Most of the students trying out had known they didn't stand a chance, but they enjoyed the opportunity to pappyshow themselves. Another girl, one of those in-between girls who wasn't quite cool but wasn't quite an outsider like herself had even asked her about it.

"Zahara, you trying out for pageant?"

The girl had looked at her and then looked at the guitar, obviously trying to make a point. Zahara had mumbled some lame excuse and ducked her head like the fooly-booly her classmates accused her of being.

"I have practice later," she had mumbled.

That was a bold-faced lie and she wasn't a good liar. She was always sure the other person could see into her heart, detect the deception. It was one of the things Granny Linda liked about her.

"I don't have to check for you," her grand-mother always said.

Zahara found it easier to tell the truth and bear the punishment, whatever it was, than the guilt and anticipation of being found out, which she inevitably was, because Granny Linda was all-seeing or something. Nothing got past her.

She practiced two extra hours that day to make up for the lie.

When she had first picked up the guitar it had been bigger than her, like if she stood behind it she might completely disappear. And for the longest while her grandmother would drive her away if she saw her so much as reach for it.

"Leave that! It's not a toy!"

But when she plucked it, sounds tumbled off of the strings and she couldn't resist the pull of it, even if it meant licks.

It was in the spare room with all the old, unused things—boxes of books, feathers, standards, and head-pieces from Carnivals past; a Singer sewing machine and a basket full of scraps. She remembered sitting on the floor near where her mother sat sewing a random piece of cloth into something beautiful. She remembered the way the machine hummed, its motor shaking the floor under her. And in the corner was the Stella Harmony.

The guitar was her father's.

She didn't know how she knew that, if she'd overheard it from her mother or Granny Linda, or if she'd just known that the one thing in the house that was untouchable belonged to the man who had been gone before she was born. She would never really know. Her mother was dead, and her grandmother, who only occasionally spoke of Zahara's mother, never ever spoke about her father. She imagined him as a heart breaker like musicians in every rock bio pic she'd ever seen.

Why else would Granny Linda seem to hate music so? Her radio was her steady companion but Granny Linda only listened to talk programmes that bored Zahara to death. As soon as the station started playing music, Granny Linda would change the station, or turn the radio off altogether.

Granny Linda didn't care for singing either. Zahara had only ever heard her grandmother sing in church.

But Granny Linda no longer went to church, although she sent Zahara like clockwork.

And it was at church, in the shadow of the gazebo that housed the statue of the Madonna, that Zahara got her first music lesson. She was seven and waiting to be called in for Holy Communion class. While the other children ran around and around the church playing some hybrid of Catch-a-Man and Freeze-a-Man, she'd sat at the sanctuary for the Lady listening to Father Ellie strum something that didn't sound like church music. Zahara was out of sight, scrunched up behind the purple bougainvillea draping itself over the gazebo. To this day, it was a mystery to her how Father Ellie had known she was there, but when the music that made her feel kind of happy-sad stopped playing, he had called to her.

"You like jazz?" he asked.

She didn't know what he meant, but it was rude not to answer an adult when spoken to and he was a Priest at that, so she found her tongue.

"I don't know jazz," she said, climbing to her feet.

He'd smiled, looking kind of happy-sad himself.

"Now you do," he said.

He patted the bench next to him and she sat. He placed the guitar, not as pretty as the Stella Harmony, on her lap. He showed her how to place her fingers under the guitar's neck just so, and guided her through the playing of her first chord ever. It was a C. A giggle had leaked out of her at the sound, surprising her.

She'd strummed the chord again and again, not tiring of the game, even when the strings started cutting into her fingers, lines of red forming at the tips. Father Ellie seemed pleased. When Ms. Adderly called them in for class, Zahara had found it hard to pay attention to the Beatitudes, rubbing her fingers where the sting felt fresh until the red lines disappeared, holding on to the feeling the music had given her.

Father Ellie became her first guitar teacher, tutoring her every Thursday before Holy Communion class. Even after she'd received the Sacrament, he had still given her lessons every Thursday, until a few years ago when he had been reassigned to a parish on another island.

Not long after that first lesson, she had started fiddling around with the guitar at home, the one no one ever played. It was out of tune and was missing some strings. Back then, she hadn't yet got the hang of tuning, but she'd saved up for a pack of new strings from Mike's Music Shop anyway. She'd plucked away, turning the pegs, until it sounded kind of okay.

"Ent I tell you leave that thing," her grandmother said when she finally caught her. She looked up from the floor, not even feeling guilty about being found out.

"Granny, listen to this," she said.

Granny Linda made her 'I'm not a Granny' face. She hated being called Granny. Zahara couldn't see how saying "Granny Linda" was any different to saying just "Granny", but it mattered to her grandmother. Normally she would have stammered an apology but she was too excited. She started plucking out a song Father Ellie had taught her. He'd said the song was about heartbreak and defiance, accepting life as it was, regretting nothing. She hadn't quite known what he meant and she couldn't quite play it right. The song had a lot more chords than she knew, but she felt kind of proud of herself anyway. She'd worked really hard on it and could hear an echo of what he'd played.

She didn't like being an echo of her mother, but with music she felt like she could make herself more solid, more real, more than just a weak not-quite-good enough understudy to a star. She couldn't ever change who she was, what she looked like, or the fact that her mother was gone, but with practice, she could get better at playing the guitar. She felt a certain power in that. And so she played the song, and looked up at her

9

grandmother, hoping she'd hear that there was some-thing more there too. Granny Linda had only stared at her, and every time her lips moved Zahara had been certain she was about to say "no." But then she'd only grunted a "hmm" and left the room.

After that, Zahara took the guitar to her room and there it stayed, propped up in the space between her bed and dresser where she could reach for it before bed, on waking, and every spare moment in between.

Granny Linda never asked about the guitar. When she started high school, Father Ellie introduced her to Mr. Patrick, the music teacher at school and church choir director. Mr. Patrick agreed to continue her les-sons after the priest left. Granny Linda didn't object to that either.

"So, wha' kinda music you like play?"

And he waited for an answer to that one, the pause stretching as he strolled beside her. So she shrugged. He smiled and nodded, as though she'd giv-en him an actual answer. Maybe she had.

Chapter 2

They called him Zulu, said he was "Africa black." The name was initially meant to insult but as often happened on the block, he'd come to own it.

He learned early that you better take your grinding or it would break you. They all understood that: Accident, Big Head, Scaly, Kong, and Monkey-See-Monkey-Do, now just called Monkey. That was his crew, the guys he'd started running with when he was just a little boy and still ran with now that they were all teenagers. They were the guys he'd learned to freestyle with until they'd eventually formed their own rap and dance crew; strong, indestructible, like Bob Marley's "Iron Lion Zion," the Lion Crew.

"Boy, pull up you pant," his grandfather bellowed often now when Zulu was leaving the house. The old man, who they called Pappy, was semi-retired. He had recently started working five days instead of seven, and so had extra time for minding his grandson's business.

He would pull up his pants, tighten the too-large belt around his waist and leave the house. When home was out of sight, he would loosen the belt and pull the pants down to where he wanted it.

"You walking like a penguin," she said.

"What?"

"You walking like a penguin," she repeated. She was giggling at him. The first words she said to him and it was mockery.

He couldn't have been happier.

The boys had been grinding him for dogging some *socie* girl who wasn't giving him the time of day.

"Patience," he'd told them.

He was giddy that his patience had paid off. He'd never had to work so hard for a hello from a girl.

"Tell you 'bout messin' with dem butter skin," Kong said.

"Feel like just cause dem brown, dem pretty," Monkey echoed, living up to his name.

"Gi me ah beautiful Nubian sistren every time," Scaly said.

They didn't understand, and he didn't feel the need to tell them, that it wasn't even about her colour. He'd been ridiculed about his skin for as long as he could remember, long enough for him to have figured out that they were all messed up in the head about something that shouldn't matter. Skin colour didn't make any one of them better than the other.

Sure, the first time someone had called him Zulu had hurt, hurt bad.

He had just started grade school and was walking home by himself for the first time. Usually, he walked hand-in-hand with his mother or got picked up by Pappy on rainy days. He'd felt like a big man with his new school bag and his Spiderman lunch kit, and had hardly felt the sun or the sweat soaking through the back of his itchy new school shirt.

They were under the tamarind tree as usual. It hardly mattered who they were, the faces changed as boys grew older. In every community on Antigua there were boys like them liming on the block somewhere. In his community, it was the tamarind tree, the one with the benches and the goat droppings underneath.

The tamarind tree was special to people of Pappy's generation, he knew that. His Pappy had lifted him up and read the sign to him once, the one affixed to the

13

tree. The sign proclaimed that the spot under the tamarind tree was where the first Prime Minister had made his most famous speech. Later he learned that the speech had practically brought down the old plantation system, helping pave the way for independence for working class people, people like Pappy, who'd driven a taxi for as long as Zulu could remember because he was determined to be his own boss.

But all that glory was long gone now. All that was left of the once resounding oratory that had inspired the workers to put down cutlass and bill was a neglected tree that smelled of piss, goat, and unwashed skin.

"Hey, hey, Zulu!"

He'd kept his head up and continued walking like his mother had instructed him to do. Later, he'd asked Pappy about it like he always did when he didn't feel comfortable talking to his mother. Pappy was gruff, but always there for him and somehow easier to talk to.

"You goin' be tall like Pappy."

"You have his lips, black like coal."

"You are the spit of him."

That's what he'd heard all his life. It always made him swell up with pride because as old as he was, Pappy was the biggest, most fearless man he knew.

14

He and Pappy had another thing in common: their love of music. Pappy played his old calypso and jazz records every Saturday telling him stories about the songs and the artistes in between the notes.

So it seemed natural in those first days of primary school to ask him, "What's a Zulu?"

He never doubted that Pappy would know. Back then he still believed Pappy knew everything.

"Where you hear that?"

"The boys under the tamarind tree," he'd mumbled.

"Hey," Pappy's voice was sharp. "Nuh hang you head. You na kill nobody. Only criminals suppose to hang dem head."

His head had snapped upwards as if pulled by a string. He and Pappy stared at each other for a long moment. Finally, Pappy rose from his chair, the lounging chair no one else in the house was allowed to sit in. He put on his white gloves, stooped before the records cabinet, and pulled out one of his prized vinyls. He walked to the old-time record player. It was a wind-up model and Zulu didn't know anyone else who owned one like it. Pappy slipped the thin black disc into place. Zulu cranked the handle, the only thing he was allowed to do.

That record player was old, older than Pappy him-self, and only old records could be played on it. For newer music, Pappy had a tape deck which was only slightly less dated. He had CDs in his taxi. According to him, this was mostly for the pleasure of the tourists he drove. But the CDs had old music too; so Zulu be-lieved that they were mostly for his pleasure as well. Pappy didn't rate new music.

This one he played though was familiar.

"I know that. That's "The Lion Sleeps Tonight" from *The Lion King*!" Zulu exclaimed.

His grandfather had laughed then.

"Not quite, Peter," he said. "This song is "Mbube" by Miriam Makeba."

He'd giggled at the funny sounding words but his grandfather had continued, "It's the traditional Zulu song that inspired the Lion King song."

"A Zulu song?"

"Yes. Zulu."

The way his grandfather said the word then it was like he wasn't talking about a far-off tribe in Africa anymore but about the boy right in front of him. It was if he was one of the Zulu people now. It was an unset-tling moment and at the same time something shifted in him. The name began to feel like something he should be happy to claim, if for no other reason than his grandfather thought so.

They didn't exchange many more words after that. Pappy just settled back down in his chair and closed his eyes, his lips curving into a smile. His fingers tapped the side of the chair, keeping time with the music as Mama Africa sang.

Months later, they were watching late night TV and happened upon an old movie about Shaka Zulu, the South African warrior king, fighting the British. He had looked at Pappy and wondered if he remembered their talk and if he saw anything of the fierce warrior in the still skinny youth at his feet. By then, Zulu had been at grade school long enough to amass his own Crew. He didn't feel as afraid and alone as he once did when passing the bullies under tamarind tree. He found there was strength in numbers, in belonging. His crew were the brothers he didn't have.

And now he was proud of the name Zulu.

So he couldn't say why, when she asked him his name, he said, "Shaka."

Chapter 3

She sometimes found herself humming her favourite part of "Trench Town Rock." It wasn't her favourite Marley song, but it was very right about music healing even before the pain.

Favourite lyrics aside, in a Bob song, it was usually the music and vibe more so than the lyrics, beautiful though they were, that put her in a mellow mood when she got herself wound up—the soothing wa-da-da-da sound the I-Threes made in the breaks on "Easy Skanking" or the wailing "whooo" they opened with on "No Woman No Cry" and then dropped in again during Tosh's wicked guitar solo about two thirds of the way through.

Lyrically speaking, she was more of a Buju than a Bob girl, which she knew to old heads would probably sound like musical blasphemy. But whatever. Buju's lyrics ran deep, especially everything on *'Til Shiloh* and a lot of the music he'd released before he went to prison. But she'd cut her teeth on Bob. If there was anything Father Ellie liked more than jazz and blues, it was old school reggae.

"It's not old school to me," he'd say. "To an Irish youth attending seminary in London in the seventies, it was just music, and the kind of music that called to the rebel in him."

That was the thing that always fascinated her about things that seemed weathered, how once upon a time they'd been brand new. Her grandmother had been brand new once. The old dresses that her mother had sewn and that she now wore because maxi dresses with bold prints were once again in style had been new once too. She never felt fully comfortable in those dresses. For one thing they dwarfed her. For another, it felt like she was wearing the hand-me-downs of someone far bolder and more interesting than she would ever be. But they were among the few fashionable clothes she owned; Granny Linda was a waste-not-want-not kind of woman. The dress she was wearing today was brown and blue, and swirly, like a lava lamp.

"You look nice," Shaka said.

She was surprised to see him there, and not just because of the too-large tie and the fact that his pants were belted around his waist so he wasn't shuffling like a penguin. She was used to him by now. He'd got into the habit of breaking off from his boys and walking her from school or music practice as far as the bus station. But here he was as she walked uphill toward the Catholic Church. She'd never seen him at her church before, not at a single Holy Communion or Confirmation class.

"You go here?" she asked, surprising herself.

"No, but you do," he said as though that explained why he was there.

It confounded her. *Would he get up early on a Sunday to come to her church just because he knew she would be there?* That seemed extreme, but she wasn't an authority on what boys thought was extreme.

"Can I carry the guitar for you?" he asked.

She'd been practicing with the youth choir for some time since Mr. Patrick, had convinced her to join. This was to be her first Sunday playing with them during mass. *Had she told him that?* As she considered the possibility that he'd come out to support her knowing she would be nervous, she blushed, embarrassed, and not even sure why.

20

Accompanying the choir, the youngest member and the only girl in the band, felt weird. Her thumb brushed lightly over the strings, keeping the rhythm while trying to blend into the wall of sound: the drum bouncing off the white walls, the red electric guitar whining 'look-at-me,' the cymbals crashing in periodically like a punctuation mark, the bass line that she shadowed as though if she stayed close enough to it no one would hear her.

"You sounded good," he said.

She knew that had to be a lie. She was sure no one had even heard her.

It was only fair that she repay him by attending one of his performances.

The Lion Crew was performing at his school's annual fête. Last week, when he'd asked her to come, she'd said "maybe." Now that he'd come out to support her first performance with the choir, the "maybe" had become a "yes." Now she just had to convince Granny Linda to let her go.

She wasn't sure how her grandmother would feel about her going to a fête. She'd never been to one before.

"Granny Linda, may I go to the Hope School fête?"

Granny was in the kitchen making fungee at the time, sweating and leaning into the task.

"What?" she asked, distracted.

"The annual Hope School fête, can I go?"

Her grandmother went quiet. She continued turning the corn meal.

Zahara waited.

"Are you playing or something?" Granny Linda asked when she finally spoke.

Granny Linda didn't encourage her guitar playing, but she didn't discourage it either; it just was. Although her grandmother didn't come right out and say it, Zahara knew that whatever Granny's Linda's relationship with God, she was proud that her granddaughter was now playing in church.

It would have been smarter to lie. Her grandmother would probably give her permission if she was performing.

"No," Zahara said.

More of the drawn-out silence, the turn stick licking against the side of the pot. She'd received licks with that stick once. Not that her grandmother was the beating type; her silences and words were usually sufficient.

Only on one occasion had Granny Linda gone too far. That was the time Zahara had broken the silver necklace, the one Granny Linda had taken from her mother's jewellery box saying that it perfectly complemented her white Holy Communion dress. When Zahara broke it, Granny Linda had snapped.

It was her worst beating in living memory. Granny Linda hadn't beaten her since, as though her grandmother had been scarred by how angry she'd been.

Zahara had heard her grandmother crying that night, and that had made her more afraid than the beating. She associated her grandmother with solid things, things not even a hurricane could knock down, like a mountain. You could strip it clean but it would go on standing. She knew that Granny Linda considered tears a weakness. Zahara didn't know how to make sense of a world in which Granny Linda was weak enough to cry. She pretended that whole memory away, the Holy Communion, the lost necklace, the beating, and the tears. She looked at her grandmother, solid in that moment, turning the cornmeal and avoiding her granddaughter's eyes.

Granny Linda didn't say anything further about her request to go to the fête. But later, as they ate the ball of fungee with a chop-up of okra, cassi, spinach, and fried snapper, Zahara eating the tail and her grandmother eating the head, Granny Linda muttered to herself.

"I suppose it was bound to happen."

Zahara pretended to be too preoccupied to notice. It wasn't a stretch. She had a history of fish bones getting stuck in her throat and she was working her way through the snapper.

She thought about the entire conversation later though, as she strummed something from the church's music catalogue, practicing for next Sunday. If her grandmother hadn't wanted her to go, she would have said so.

She went.

Her fingers itched for her guitar as she waited for the show to start. The auditorium was loud and busy, bodies moving around, girls in groups, guys edging up to girls. Quiet in the midst of it all, she felt what Father Ellie had described during one of their music lessons as *dal niente*, that moment of stillness, of suspended expectation, before launching into an ear-splitting *crescendo*.

"You came," Shaka said and when she turned, there he was looking like himself in a white t-shirt and low-slung jeans. Somehow she'd thought he'd wear leather or something, something flashy for the stage.

She would soon learn that he didn't need all that. His rapping was one thing, a flow that reminded her of Mos Def, kind of mumbling and deep, but his dancing was another. He moved like a snake, as if his body didn't have any bones. The Lion Crew was dancing to the music. According to their hype man—a tall, husky boy who introduced himself as Kong—they had mixed the beat together themselves. It was an unusual mix of standard hip-hop with samples of the UB40 version of "I Got You Babe," Lauryn Hill's version of "Can't Take My Eyes Off of You," and Buju Banton's "Love Sponge." Unusual choices unless you were as into music as she was; and somehow she knew it was all him. Had she mentioned to him how much Buju's music meant to her? It felt like the mix was made just for her, especially when he gave her the CD afterwards.

"Thank you," she said. "You guys were good."

That's when he introduced her to his boys. They laughed when she called him 'Shaka', but stifled it when he glared at them.

She listened to the CD that night in her Discman, remembering the way he'd moved under the lights.

The next time she came upon him waiting for her by the school gate as he'd taken to doing, she was the first to talk, breaking with the rhythm of their previous exchanges in which he had worked to pull every response out of her.

"I liked the mix," she said.

The smile he gave in response was shy.

His expression was shyer still when he took her hand several meetings later and led her off their usual path and toward the Botanical Gardens. She knew that the Gardens were run down and abandoned and mostly used as an after-school lovers' lane. She thought about resisting, conversations she'd overheard at school about boys taking every little encouragement as a go-ahead surging forward in her mind. She liked Shaka and looked forward to their daily meet-up. She considered his walking her from school to the bus stop part of their routine. But she wasn't interested in anything else, and if he thought she was, well he hadn't learned anything about her.

"Relax," he said, as though he had heard her thoughts.

She knew that she was projecting her thoughts loudly and she had learned that he was the kind of boy who listened not only to the things she said, but the things she didn't. He would have felt the tensing of her hand, and could no doubt feel the way she relaxed, although only marginally, at his reassurance. Mostly, she agreed to the detour because she was curious and she knew he wouldn't push her to do anything she didn't want to.

She'd gotten pretty good at reading him too.

When they walked through the gate of the Gardens, he didn't try to pull her off into some overgrown corner. No, they sat right there on the roots of the huge ficus, private but not hidden. He took a breath then reached into his battered backpack. He pulled out a digital recorder so small he could close his palm around it, and placed it in her hand. She looked at him in confusion but stuck the buds in her ears and pressed the start button. It was his voice and his words coming out of the recorder; no music, no percussion apart from that provided by the natural rhythm of his flow.

She looked at him but he was deliberately looking away at nothing in particular. She smiled. She pictured him in some quiet place saying words as they came to him into the recording device; the way he sometimes stopped and started over or made insertions made it clear that this was him just working it out. She knew instinctively that nobody ever got to hear his verses when they were this fresh. She understood that it mattered to him that she got him; remembered him saying one time that as much as he liked rapping and dancing, writing was his favourite thing, but not exactly the kind of thing he could showboat about. Not even among his boys who would grind him on principle.

She closed her eyes, and her body leaned in to the rhythm of his voice. She didn't come back to herself until he touched her arm.

"Time to go," he said.

She still had to catch the bus. She started to hand over the recorder.

"Keep it til you finish," he said, standing.

She smiled and didn't resist when he took her hand again as they walked out of the Gardens.

Zahara logged in to Skype. Her school had received new computer labs under the government's Bridging the Digital Divide programme, and she'd been able to reconnect with her musical mentor, Father Ellie. She'd learned he wasn't that far away, just up North, in Jamaica. He was happy to hear from her and pleased to learn that she was still playing the guitar. But right then he wasn't online. And she really, really needed to tell someone.

"I met a boy," she typed.

Chapter 4

"So, ah you gyal now?" Kong asked.

It was near dusk and they were idling on the basketball court. Because of the "Be Home by Dark" rule, they would have to head out soon.

Shaka shrugged. Even though she wasn't there, he didn't want to be putting words into her mouth.

"Yeah, me guess she alright," Kong said, as though giving his blessing.

Shaka laughed.

"Thanks for your approval, Oh Mighty Kong," and all the boys laughed, Shaka too, remembering how Kong had come to have that particular nickname.

They'd been eleven years old or so, bored and maybe a little sun-crazy one long hot summer. Mango-bearing season had come and gone, so there were no trees worth climbing. They hadn't had enough money between them to buy the Play Station they'd been eyeing at Courts, and they didn't dare steal it as Kong had suggested.

He wouldn't stop griping about it.

"Bunch ah cowards."

"Oh, please, like you'd ah done it! You always ah chat!" Shaka had said.

Before long he and Kong were stalking each other, sizing each other up for a fight.

"You think yuh bad?"

"You think yuh bad?"

That kind of thing.

Then Shaka had dared the boy who would later become Kong, to lift Pappy's car.

"Since you feel you so bad," he taunted.

That Kong had even attempted it can only be attributed to how hot it was and how bored they were.

The car had been jacked up on blocks for repair work for two weeks and Pappy had been in a foul mood the whole time. Unable to work, he had no doubt been feeling like somebody had ripped a hole in his pocket. For Shaka and his friends, the stationary car had become just another place to play until Pappy ran them off every fifteen minutes or so.

Kong, already taller and bigger than the rest of them, flexed his muscles, dipped his knees, leaned his whole body into the task, and lifted the black Lincoln Town Car. Maybe the blocks had shifted or something, but no sooner had he lifted it than it came crashing down with a loud *bap*! They were all frozen in shock, mouths open, hearts hammering, eyes bugging out, frozen except for Kong who had howled like Banshee in the X-men comics or a werewolf during full moon.

Kong's howling had brought Pappy running from the living room where he'd camped out in his lounging chair as he usually did when he wasn't working. He was apoplectic, a word Shaka would later learn, and when he did, he would remember that moment, how Pappy's head had seemed to explode, his mouth guppying as words stuck in his throat. Only a squeak came out, the kind of sound no grown man should make, a squeak, like air escaping a balloon. And like the balloon Pappy was deflating right before their eyes until finally, he had sat at the side of the road, the wind knocked out of him.

No amount of apologizing could've spared them.

After that incident, his mother had started sending him to the community radio station just one road up from their home.

"Time for you to learn a trade, keep you out of trouble," she'd said. She'd asked a friend of a cousin of hers who worked there to "give him something to do" and told him to "behave" or else she'd hear about it.

He hadn't seen it as punishment though. Not when he got to be around all that music. The men at the station talked about music all the time, and they had treated him like he was one of them.

"How you mean Tosh better than Marley? You better wheel and come again!"

"Marley min weak, jack, ah sing all kind ah love song while Tosh ah tear dung Babylon."

It felt like an old argument, although it was new to him. He and his friends often had arguments about who was the greatest hip-hop artiste of all time: Tupac, Jay Z, or his personal favourite, Nas.

At the station, he'd felt like he was swimming in music and he absolutely loved it. Every day, as fast as he could, he would burn CDs, until he had all but copied the radio station's music library to his own. And by the time he'd brought home a live recording of Nina Simone singing "Go to Hell," Pappy had forgiven him. By then Pappy had also bought a new car, thanks to his insurance.

It was at the station that he had first learned to mix. Diva, a DJ with a bass drum of a voice and locs so long she had to loop them into a triple ponytail, had caught him copying *Ella in Berlin*. Ella Fitzgerald wasn't one of Pappy's favourites; his grandfather preferred more tortured blues, like Billie Holiday, but Shaka quite liked Ella's joyful live rendition of "Mack the Knife."

"Little man, wha' you know 'bout Ella?" Diva had teased instead of reporting him.

She'd started showing him the ropes and they still talked and swapped music to this day.

As for Kong, when he'd dropped the car, the blocks holding up the right back end had fallen onto his foot. It never healed properly and so he still walked with a limp, or as he liked to call it, a 'bop'. Plus, Pappy had said he couldn't come around anymore, which Shaka figured wasn't strictly fair since he was the one who'd dared his friend to lift the car. It was perhaps the injustice of it that had made the Crew accept the nick-name. It was a name Kong had chosen for himself, figuring he would rather be known for being strong like King Kong than being called 'Sore Foot' or "Elephant Man' because of his limp.

Chapter 5

"I like playing all kinds," she volunteered.

They'd been walking in silence, her with the guitar slung over her shoulder, him bopping along beside her, a now familiar routine. She wouldn't let him carry the guitar although he always offered.

The look on his face told her that he had no idea what she was talking about. She looked at him out of the corner of her eye, slightly impatient.

"You asked me what kind of music I liked playing," she said.

His eyebrows rose to his hairline.

"Weeks and weeks ago," he replied.

She shrugged.

"Well I thought about it, and I like all kinds."

"All kind like what?"

She shrugged again.

"Okay," he said. "How 'bout this? You gi me one, I gi you one, you gi me one, I gi you one, like that 'til we done."

She didn't answer.

"Kanye West," he said.

"Bob Marley," she said, after a pause.

He looked disappointed.

"Everybody like Bob," he said. "That na tell me nothing. Okay, Lauryn Hill."

"Lauryn Hill," she said.

"Now you playing with me," he protested.

She flashed him a sweet little smile. She was enjoying herself.

"Roland Prince," he said.

She was surprised he even knew who that was. Her expression must have showed as much because he laughed.

"What?" he said. "One of the top jazz guitarists in the world, and he from Wadadli. You think I wouldn't know that? How ignorant you think me be?"

She was a little ashamed of herself for thinking that his knowledge would be limited to rap and reggae. After all his music knowledge was part of what had intrigued her. She'd have to step up her game, maybe show him she knew a little about his world.

"Common …no, wait, Gil Scott-Heron," she said, and he smiled and nodded as if to say, "Good one."

"Amy Winehouse…no wait, Janis Joplin," he said.

She didn't like to think about the similarities between the two rock goddesses beyond their obvious talent. She decided to lighten things up.

"Wiz Khalifa."

"Adam Levine."

"Maroon Five."

"No fair," he teased, and she found herself giggling, an honest-to-goodness giggle as if he'd tickled her.

"Hey, you like Hendrix?" he asked. She arched her eyebrows and he laughed.

"Every guitar player likes Hendrix," she said.

"I have 'Are You Experienced' on vinyl," he said. "You wan' hear it?"

He invited her to his house to do just that. He told her how, when he got home from school, his Pappy and his mother would still be at work, and that it was his job to get dinner started in between doing his homework. He wasn't allowed to go out until his mother or Pappy got home from work unless he had a shift at the station.

"Does your mom call the station to check up on you?" she asked.

"Nah, not really," he said, adding, "when I first started, I was still little and, you know how it is, somebody would always report you if you did anything outta the way. But she trust me now, man. Besides, I have cover."

"Cover?" she asked.

"Yes, Diva, one of the best DJs there, and one of my best friends since I was 'bout eleven."

She started to say how she couldn't imagine being friends with an adult, but then remembered Father Ellie and how she thought of him as her friend.

"Hey, no need to be jealous," he teased, no doubt deliberately misreading her silence. "Me only have eyes for one girl."

He could never pass up an opportunity to flirt. She was getting used to it. She rolled her eyes.

"So, it'd be cool then?" she asked returning to the point. She really wanted to hear the original Hendrix recording if he actually had it.

"Well, there's still the nosy neighbours, always some of those," he said, but he didn't seem too bothered, and it wasn't like they were going to be doing anything wrong.

So rather than taking the bus home as she normally would, she walked with him to his house and allowed him to sneak her in. It felt like sneaking, but maybe just because she knew no adults were there, that they'd be well and truly alone.

He immediately went to the wooden music cabinet in the living room, digging around for the record. She could see he was trying his best to act normal, like it was no big deal that she was there. He found the record and she watched, fascinated, as he lifted it carefully from its sleeve, his tongue between his teeth in concentration as he slipped it gently into place and began cranking up the player that was unlike anything she'd seen before.

The record spun and music started. She reclined in Pappy's chair and closed her eyes, fingers instinctively feeling for the music as her lips mouthed the familiar words to "Wind Cries Mary," one of the pioneer rock guitarist's more soulful tracks.

Shaka sat a safe distance and though her eyes were closed, she could feel him watching her.

After the record had spun through "Red House," "Joe," and the title track "I Don't Live Today" at least once, she opened her eyes to find him smiling at her.

"What?" she asked, self-conscious.

"What what?" he teased, his smile now a big-teeth grin.

"You smiling at me."

"Yeah, people do that when dem happy," he said.

No shyness about him at all.

"Music makes me happy," she said, smiling now.

He gave her a 'no kidding' look and she laughed.

"Pappy ah wan dinosaur when it come to music – mostly jazz and blues, soul, some early rock, some he consider in a class by themselves like Jimi – but truth is some ah me happiest and earliest memories come from sitting right here soaking all this up."

He waved a hand at the cabinet filled with records.

"My father was dead and my mother had to work all the time, but Pappy being here and sharing this with me made me feel…" At that he paused. He almost looked shy.

"Feel?" she pushed.

His eyes ducked. "Safe, loved."

His bond with his grandfather wasn't news to her, nor was the fact that his father was dead. The former was obvious from how often Shaka dropped "Pappy" into conversation; the latter he'd mentioned only once, in an offhand way, like it was no big deal. And she supposed, with him having always had Pappy, maybe it wasn't.

"I think my father played guitar," she said.

"Yeah?"

She didn't talk casually about her mother or father.

"I don't really know who he is…but yeah, I think so," she said. She shrugged. "Is just a feeling."

He nodded.

"Well, the talent have to come from somewhere, right?"

And since that was pretty much her thinking, too, she just nodded. Sharing that small suspicion, which she had no way of ever confirming, felt like a huge leap for her.

"Where you coming from?" Granny Linda demanded as she slipped into the house much later. Her grandmother didn't wait for an answer; she just turned away, muttering loud enough for Zahara to hear.

"Don't start thinking you're a big woman, coming in here as you feel like."

Chapter 6

A melody that was sort of a mix of Pharrell's "Happy" and Set On's "Smiles a Lot" looped together in his head as he walked home from escorting her to the nearest bus stop. There was some Katarina and the Waves "Walking on Sunshine" in there as well, and he knew he must look silly bopping his head to nothing but he couldn't bring himself to care.

He rhymed over the music in his head, holding on to the words until he could get back home and get his hands on a notebook or his laptop. She hadn't returned his digital recorder yet, hadn't said anything about his rhymes either. He was trying not to ask. She did things in her own time, as he'd learned by how long it had taken her to acknowledge his existence in the beginning.

A few days later, she finally played for him, singing along, albeit very, very softly, with the guitar. They were sitting again on the roots of the ficus in the Botanical Gardens. He thought she sounded like Sade or like the honey and rum mixture Pappy had once given him when his throat was scratchy from a cold. Pappy had added lime to dilute the rum, but his mother had still complained. He hadn't, as she'd feared, developed a taste for rum, although he had since nipped a bit from his grandfather's stash. The rum burned when he drank it by itself; but the delectable mix of rum, honey, and lime soothed. That's how she sounded, soulful, soothing.

He recognized the words right away as his, from one of his rhymes, but with the melody she'd created they sounded so different. He couldn't do anything but sit there with his mouth open. He tried to find something intelligent to say, something more intelligent than the big smile spreading across his face.

"That's mine," he said.

She placed the guitar in rest position across her lap and leaned back against the tree trunk. They just sat there, smiling at each other, alone except for the vagrant sleeping some yards away on a bench.

It was early, before school. Last night she'd texted him to meet her in the Gardens and he'd readily agreed.

His mother usually had to harass him to get out of bed, and she had given him the side eye when he'd come into the kitchen dressed in his uniform before the usual time. But she'd said nothing, probably relieved to have him up and out of the house without a fuss. The boys would have words for him later.

They'd gotten used to him ditching them in the afternoons to walk her to the stop, but the mornings were still theirs. It couldn't be helped though.

When he'd arrived there, she'd been waiting, guitar in her lap, her pleated jumper covering her knees. She'd seemed nervous and when she began playing without preamble, he'd understood why.

The song was from his rhyme "Hip Chick." He'd written it when he'd first spotted her walking home from school. In the opening lines, he wondered how he'd never seen her before, if his eyes had been clouded, if he had early onset of cataracts. The chorus went on to thank God for letting an angel walk across his vision…and other cheesy crap that somehow became lyrical gold when she sang it.

He wondered if she knew she'd inspired it. Usually he didn't write about girls; that had been done and done. He wanted to be out of the box, like Nas. So, he wrote about other things. He'd once written a whole series of raps about colours and how they reflected his moods. Orange. Sunset. Red. Hibiscus. Blue. The Sky. The kind of stuff he couldn't share with the boys because they expected him to write 'big batty' rhymes.

"Yeah it's your song," she said. "You have skills…but you could dig deeper."

His smile faded. For the first time, he found he was disenchanted with her. None of her silences had irritated him as much as her dissing his verse.

"Wey mi recorder?" he demanded.

She dug into her messenger bag, handed over the small device. He stuffed it into his backpack.

"Let's write something together," she offered.

He choopsed.

Why would she want to write something with someone she thought had no talent? he wondered. Who said she had any talent with the way she played like she didn't want anybody to hear? For all he knew she was as shallow as any other girl he'd come across, she just pretended better. She didn't have any right to be dissing his work.

She smiled, and in spite of himself, he felt stupid.

"It's just that…" she hesitated. "I feel things when I read your lines and I wonder how much more powerful that feeling could be if your writing wasn't so …self-conscious."

He zipped up his backpack and said nothing, but he was listening.

"I know something 'bout that," she went on quietly. "I live there."

He'd never thought of himself as hiding, not the way she did. He didn't like to think of himself that way. But he did like the idea of creating something with her. It might be fun.

He wasn't ready to tell her so yet, though.

No one had ever made him doubt his writing the way she had. He needed time for that to settle. Then, maybe.

"Maybe," he said.

And she nodded.

Chapter 7

She tried not to read too much into the fact that he hadn't said anything good, bad, or indifferent about her music. Outside of lessons, she'd never played for just one person before. And she'd never sung for anyone besides him. She felt exposed.

Whenever she was tense like she was now, music helped. So she put in her Claudette 'CP' Peters CD, turned off the lights, and danced, brukking out to "I'm in Control" wishing she felt half as confident as the soca diva sounded.

She bet he would be surprised to know that CP was one of her favourite artistes, that she enjoyed watching her on TV during the Party Monarch, the way she owned the audience for the three or so minutes of her performance. And if she could meet CP she'd ask her, "how do you do it?"

"Do what?" CP might say, throwing her red locs over her shoulder, the expression on her face quizzical but still kind.

"How are you so confident?"

Because the woman really was like a superhero to her, like Storm or the Black Widow. Zahara was fascinated by the way she moved across the stage, it was like she could smite you as soon as look at you and wear a head-to-toe cat suit while doing it. In fantasy, Zahara wanted to be like her; to have an alter ego she could slip on or off, depending on the circumstances.

"I'm not confident," CP might say, like she was sharing an inside secret. "I'm just good at faking it."

Zahara wondered if maybe all performers were like that. She'd seen Prince's performances; how wantonly he played and sang like he was stripping the lyrics naked. She'd, also, seen his interviews, the way he blushed and stuttered, stirring a kinship in her. Jimi was like that, too. Maybe they were all like that, even CP. Maybe away from the bright lights, those celebrities danced in their rooms in the dark too.

At school the next day, her class watched the documentary *Dark Girls*. She'd seen it already when it showed on Oprah's network but she didn't mind watching it again. Some of the other girls fidgeted and sighed in boredom, or maybe it just made them uncomfortable.

"I hope you were paying attention," said Mrs. Keener, the Social Sciences teacher, as the closing credits rolled on the screen. "Your report for over the break is on colourism or shadeism in the Caribbean."

"What's that, Miss?" someone piped up. It was Cathy, the girl they called 'Chatty Cathy' because she was so talkative. The other girls snickered.

"Well, Cathy," Mrs. Keener said, clearly not amused. "The fact that you weren't paying attention means more work for you over the summer. This project will be worth at least forty percent of your Social Sciences' grade next year, because yes, you will be having me again next year. So if you're thinking of blowing it off, think again."

That shut everybody up, everybody except Cathy.

"Miss, that's not fair. Summer is summer. You can't give us homework over summer."

"I just did," Mrs. Keener said ignoring the groaning and begging that rose around the classroom.

She turned to the board and wrote out the project details. It was clear that the discussion was closed.

That night, Zahara found herself listening to Buju's "Love Me Browning," the song in which he declared his love for light-skinned women. That song had sparked so much controversy that he'd written another one, "Love Black Women." She listened to that song too, singing along with the words.

She texted Shaka.

Did u liik me bcuz Im liit?

He didn't answer right away, and for a moment she thought he might not, that maybe he was still mad at her for being honest with him about his songs. She worried that she'd been too blunt. She did like his rhymes but she thought he was capable of so much more. That's what she'd been trying to tell him, but it seemed that she was coming off the wrong way. She had never been very good at explaining herself. Now she wondered if she'd chased away the first guy that liked her.

Her phone buzzed.

It was something of a miracle that she even had a cell. Their house wasn't a very tech-savvy one. There was a single TV in the living room. She owned a Discman because she'd managed to convince Granny Linda that she needed it for her music lessons. That wasn't a lie. She needed to listen to music to practice and she preferred the full album experience over downloading singles. It was a bonus that a Discman was cheaper than an iPod.

Her first cell phone had been a Christmas gift from Granny Linda's sister, the one who lived in St. Croix and treated them like a charity case during her infrequent visits. Granny Linda had taken the shiny, new phone away, claiming it didn't sync up with any of the local service providers, whatever that meant. She'd got Zahara a new cell, and Zahara had chosen not to look a gift horse in the mouth.

She was pretty sure her Granny hadn't meant for her to use it to talk to boys after dark, although she wondered if Granny Linda even remembered that she had it.

"Hi," she said, softly.

"Hi," he said.

There was a long silence.

"Are you still mad?" she asked finally.

"No."

"You still sound vex," she said.

"I'm not. Let it go."

She shut up.

"Your text-speak sucks," he said. "Wha' you min ah try say?"

Yes, he was definitely still mad.

"I was asking if my colour had anything to do with why you noticed me."

He wooshed through his mouth.

"I don't know. Guess so, likkle bit."

She was surprised he'd admitted it.

"Really?"

"Really," he said. "You wan' say *my* colour didn't have nothing to do with why you gave me such a hard time?"

"It didn't…wait; I didn't give you a hard time."

He laughed. It was good to hear his laugh again.

"Stop lie," he said.

"I don't," she insisted, though she wasn't as certain of that as she'd once been. After all, she was lying to Granny Linda about where she went when she met up with him. She didn't tell direct lies but weren't they still lies?

She thought seriously about his question. Was his dark skin the reason she'd been reluctant to pay attention to him at first?

No, she decided, she hadn't been lying.

A few weeks ago, before he'd first started checking for her, she wouldn't have given any boy the time of

51

day. First of all, she was shy. Secondly, there was Granny Linda. Third, her entire world up until then had been about school and music. Fourth, Granny Linda. Fifth, she just didn't think that boys would be checking for her.

She saw the girls in school and how they'd blossomed. She knew that she hadn't developed in the same way. She didn't think she was beautiful. It was funny, because her mother had been beautiful. But if she imagined her mother's features on her face, they just seemed to fall flat. There was a spark in her mother's eyes that she didn't see in her own. As if the charm that had touched her mother had danced right past her.

It didn't make sense to her that a guy would look at her, butter-skin or not. She was nothing special to look at. And once she realized that he wasn't playing a joke on her, that he really liked her, it made even less sense.

She thought he was magnificent, and it had nothing to do with his colour. It was his eyes that always seemed to have a smile in them and the way his features were arranged in a uniquely impish way so that he always seemed like he was pulling her leg. It was the way he moved his long, lean body, as if to the beat of an internal rhythm.

Chapter 8

He'd been selected to play Anansi, the trickster spider in a stage adaptation of Ashley Bryan's *The Dancing Granny*. The play would be enacted by the youth theatre, part of a Culture Department summer programme.

He figured his dancing skills had something to do with him getting the leading role since the play was a musical. Making his body do just what he wanted it to had always come easily to him, whether it was dancing or on the basketball court. Dancing was something he could do without even thinking about it. He liked how he felt doing it too, charged, like lightning was pulsing through his body. Still, a theatre production wasn't the kind of thing he usually went out for.

His English teacher, Mr. Perry, was directing it. Mr. Perry had seen him dance in the school pageant and had personally approached him about the Anansi role. He figured it wouldn't hurt to get on the teacher's good side.

"Suck up," Kong accused.

And Shaka couldn't deny it.

When he told Zahara, during one of their walks home from school, her lips quirked and he made a motion with his hands as if to say, go ahead get it out of your system. She laughed and laughed. He'd never heard her laugh so fully. And at first it was beautiful to see her laugh like that, so freely. He laughed with her, but the longer it went on, the more his nerves about taking on the part and his memory of her criticism of his writing crept in.

"You ah mock me?" he asked, trying to play it off like it wasn't a serious question.

But the way she sobered up and stopped walking right away told him she'd heard the insecurity in his voice. He stopped, too, turned fully toward her and could read the truth in her eyes when she said, "No, I think you'll make a great Anansi."

Still…

"What then?"

Her lips quirked again, but her eyes were teasing gently. She shrugged.

"Just got a picture in my head of you dancing around as a crafty, impish, always-up-to-something Anansi," and she kind of wiggled her body as she said this so that he was laughing again too.

He decided to show her how it's really done. He gave her some of his best moves, dancing around her, not caring that traffic and other people were going by, continuing even when she blushed and laughed so hard that her face was like a ripe plum.

He got her back by recommending her for the live band Mr. Perry wanted for the production. She played the guitar like it was an extension of her arm, only she didn't seem to know it. He'd realized that despite her talent and her passion for music she was timid about performing in front of people, something that came natural-natural to him; that's why she always played so softly. He thought the band would be good for her and she'd be good for the band.

"I don't even go to your school," she said.

That was true. He was at public school; she went to a private Catholic school.

"Doesn't matter," he said. "It's not a school pro-duction. Mr. Perry just wants good musicians."

And she couldn't even use her Granny Linda's strictness as an excuse. He knew by now that her grandmother didn't object to her music.

"You have skills…me na done say so?"

She blushed.

"No."

He didn't know if she was denying her skills or saying he hadn't told her. Either way, his answer was "Yes." And when he saw from her slight smile and nod that she accepted his answer, he added, with a teasing smile, "Don't want you getting a big head though."

She rolled her eyes and picked up the original thread of the conversation.

"Okay," she said. "I'll do it, but only if you…"

"I know, I know, write a song with you," he finished.

"But that's not all," she said. "I also want you to help me out with this project I have to do for school."

He frowned. "What project?"

He did okay in school, or his mother would have his tail, but he was no genius.

"I'm getting to that," she continued. "I want to do a little social experiment."

His frown deepened.

"What kind of experiment?"

Her idea was to use a cell phone video recorder like an invisible eye to investigate how skin colour affected social interactions among teens. Since she was terrible at socializing, she wanted he and some of the Lion Crew to be her on-camera guys interacting with their peers, kind of like a reality show. She would stay in the background and videotape everything that happened.

"I have a better idea," he said. "You be on camera."

"Me?" She sounded incredulous, vigorously shaking her head.

"Yes," he insisted. "Nice butter-skin like you."

"Stop it," she said, looking annoyed.

"Wha'? Gyal ah bleach out dem skin fu look lakka you." He sing-songed this in an imitation of the Buju Browning track so she'd know he was kidding.

It took a lot of convincing but finally it was agreed. The *Anansi* production would be the set of their little reality show, and she wouldn't be the only one putting herself out there; they would both be in the fish bowl. His boys would audition for roles in the production or get jobs helping out with the behind-the-scenes stuff so that they could be in place to film the action from as many angles as possible.

"Who me?" Kong said when Shaka asked him to help out. "Is summertime man, Zulu."

"Shaka," he interrupted. He'd told his boys he was going by 'Shaka' now but it was taking them some time to get used to calling him that.

"Okay, okay, *Shaka*," Kong corrected himself. "But wha' me ah say, jack, ah summertime. You think man na ha nutten fu do but help you suck up to gyal who nar even gi you nutten?"

"Ah na Crew arwe be?" Shaka asked.

Kong had no rebuttal. They were supposed to have each other's backs no matter what. That was the deal.

"Fine," Kong said grudgingly, which meant the rest of the crew was in as well. Wherever Kong went, they followed. And once Kong had signed on to the reality show idea, Shaka was surprised by how much enthusiasm his friend showed. Kong was already giving orders as they walked to the Culture Department for that first day of rehearsal.

"Mek sure you do a white balance and steady the picture before you start shooting. Mek sure you do um manually. Na trust the camera fu do um, arwe na wan' no jerky, off-colour picture."

"Frame the picture properly," Kong continued.

"All that *and* mek sure dem na see arwe a shoot? Ah joke you ah make," said Accident.

"Genius, keep de camera an' dem on. Ready an' on, an' in landscape not portrait," Kong said.

"Landscape? Portrait? Man, ah wha' you ah talk 'bout?" Big Head's head made an easy target when Kong flicked him. He turned to demonstrate how the camera worked, walking backwards as he did so.

"Landscape, portrait, landscape, portrait." Kong turned back around. "You all better recognize we live in a kinda time now where man custom to having the camera around. Dem na even notice dem no more, so you jus' stay ready," he said.

"And keep your camera on, but on silent," Shaka reminded them. He didn't want Mr. Perry banning phones altogether because somebody's ringtone interrupted practice.

"Just put the phone in airplane mode," Kong said. "That way no call or text message go come through fu bruk up the recording."

"Man, ah wey you learn all dem subben dey?" Accident asked.

"Me read the manual unlike *some* people," Kong replied.

"Ain't nobody got time for that," Scaly joked, pushing him lightly. The Lion Crew chuckled.

Zahara chuckled too. She'd been walking a little behind them; partly listening to their banter, partly trying to psyche herself up for her audition.

"Hey, we can put it up on YouTube when we done," Kong suggested. "Go viral."

Zahara coughed, almost choking on her own spit.

Shaka cut in. "Calm down. You scaring my girl."

And he smiled as Zahara had a full-on coughing fit at that.

Chapter 9

For her audition, Zahara kept it simple. She played "Jamaica Farewell."

She had learned it last term for a school production, one of those things where everybody had to participate or else. They had sung a medley of Caribbean folk songs and while she hadn't played in the production, Mr. Patrick had taught her the music. She knew it well so it didn't matter how nervous she was; her fingers remembered. Plus, Shaka had said some of the songs in the play would be set to a calypso rhythm making the classic Harry Belafonte melody a good fit for her audition.

When she finished, her armpits were sticky with sweat. She peered nervously at Mr. Perry, waiting for him to say "Thanks, I'll get back to you." She was surprised when he jumped up from his seat and vigorously shook her hand, welcoming her to the orchestra, a combo really; a keyboardist, a drummer, and herself on the guitar.

"Thanks!" she stuttered. She hadn't expected him to make his decision so quickly. The other musicians were smiling.

"We might experiment with some other rhythms," Mr. Perry told them. "So I hope you guys are game for that. Some hip-hop, some dancehall, some soca. We want this to be Anansi for the millennial generation, you feel me?"

She glanced across the room and saw Kong rolling his eyes and Shaka biting his lip to keep from laughing. She stifled a giggle. *Yeah, adults trying to talk hip were just kind of dorky-sounding.* Even she knew that.

It was weird seeing Anansi as a man, albeit a man with a wiliness of spirit and spider-like moves. But that was just how Ashley Bryan had portrayed Anansi in *The Dancing Granny.* He'd taken the legendary trickster out of fable and legend and given him a human existence complete with a wife and mother-in-law willing to look the other way on the suspicious subject of where he was getting the ground provisions he brought to their dinner table.

It was the second day of rehearsal. They were seated in a circle on the raised platform that was their temporary stage, reading and discussing the script. They were on the subject of how Anansi always seemed to get away with things; in this case because those close to him chose to look the other way.

"And don't we all know people like that?" Mr. Perry asked them. "People who are happy to partake without questioning the source?"

He explained to them that he was taking the time to discuss these issues as they had to fully understand the story. Then they would build the production from that knowledge, leaving room for adlibs and experimentation. Zahara found this unsettling but exciting.

"I want this to be an exercise in comprehension and creation," Mr. Perry said. "Artful elaboration."

Heads nodded all around the circle.

"The music too," he added, staring intently at Zahara and the other musicians. "We're building that from the ground up. What's Granny's mood as she hoes her garden that first day? How has her mood shifted by the end as she watches the wasteland that her garden has become?"

His words made Zahara think of how Granny Linda had once ripped up every last one of her pigeon peas plants in frustration over the cows and goats that came nipping at them each day. Her grandmother had taken up handfuls of the uprooted plants and dragged them down the road to Ms. Willoughby's place.

"Nothing left for them to take," she'd told an astonished Ms. Willoughby whose animals had been the cause of many upsets between her and Granny Linda.

After that, Granny Linda hadn't put on her straw hat, long dress, and old Timberland boots for weeks. Eventually, she'd returned to her garden though. It was her stress relief after days spent at her job at the Prime Minister's office, where people were usually upset by the time they got to her desk, and even more upset when she had to put them off from seeing the Prime Minister for yet another day. Granny Linda would be as taut as a guitar string about to snap by the time she got home from work. She needed her garden.

Zahara used to watch from the window as her grandmother slashed at the ground, pulling up weeds, digging for potatoes, cutting and trimming bushes until she'd either tired herself out or the day's tension had eased out of her. She'd be talking to the plants by the time she was done, and if one of them gave up something good that day—big red tomatoes for their dinner plate maybe—she'd even be smiling.

Granny Linda was grinning that time she made her take the picture, the one where her grandmother was posing with the huge, juicy watermelon. It was one of the few times she'd seen her grandmother grin like that. Granny Linda had cut up the fruit and shared it with the whole neighbourhood, even Ms. Willoughby.

The medals her grandmother won at the annual Home and Garden Show hung from the back of her bedroom door, so that there was a chorus of metal swinging against wood every time the door was opened, like a chime warning Zahara that her grandmother was coming.

So, Granny Linda, that's who she thought of as they read about the Granny in the play, though she had a hard time picturing Granny Linda dancing like the Granny in the story. The very idea made her giggle.

"What so funny?" whispered the boy sitting next to her. He was the drummer.

She shrugged.

"Danny," he said. She looked at him, quizzically.

"My name. Danny."

Had she asked his name? she wondered. Then she remembered she was supposed to be social, or at least approachable. So she gave him a stiff smile and whispered back, "Zahara."

And of course, she was the one to get caught.

"Let's have one conversation please," Mr. Perry said staring straight at her.

Danny sniggered and she wanted to turn away from him altogether. She ignored him for the rest of the session although he continued trying to catch her attention.

True to their plan, the Lion Crew had captured everything on film. Later, when she looked at the footage of her interaction with Danny it was obvious that the drummer had scoped her out. His eyes had been on her for some time before he actually spoke to her and he had checked to see where she was sitting and then sat next to her. She was the lightest girl there, and the only one who seemed to be on his radar.

She couldn't wrap her mind around being the pick. In a room of theatre geeks, many of whom were still way cooler than her, he'd singled her out. But there was no way to know for sure if it was because she was light-skinned. Maybe he was just interested in her because they were in the band together.

"It could be 'cause you're the prettiest one," Shaka suggested.

They were in his bedroom later that day, reviewing the video on his laptop. His boys had walked with them halfway to his house but they'd parted ways at the tamarind tree.

She cut her eyes at him, no fire behind it, but *really, 'the prettiest one?'*

"Yes, you are," he said. He looked straight at her.

"Of course, if you knew how pretty you are you probably wouldn't be here with me right now. So, on the one hand, good for me." He chuckled. "But on the other hand…come on…you must know how pretty you be."

She had to laugh at the two of them, trying to convince each other that they were special enough for the other. They were a case, for real; she especially so.

"You pretty," he insisted, tilting her chin toward him. She started at his touch but didn't pull away.

"Me sure bwoi min ah check fu you long time but you so deep inna yuh music, so down on yourself, you never even notice. For the record, you pretty and not cause o' no skin colour nutten neither. Just 'cause."

He kissed her then. It was her first kiss, and she had a feeling it was maybe his too. It was a little awkward, but nice. They were both shy, pulling away after the first, second, third brush of lips. His eyes darted to

67

his bedroom door, as though someone would barge in and discover them at any moment.

Perhaps they'd both feared the same thing, because when Pappy's voice called out, "Boy, you home?" they flew apart.

Shaka cleared his throat before answering, "Yes, Pappy."

She smoothed her skirt and reached for her guitar, wondering how she was going to get out of there. There was only one way out of the room, and that way led toward his grandfather's voice.

"Come on," Shaka said. She followed him out to the living room, her heartbeat racing as she prepared for the worst.

The old man's eyebrows curled together when he saw them, but then his eyes danced as if he didn't know whether to chastise Shaka or pat him on the back.

"What you doin' lock up in your room with girl?" he asked, gruffly.

She couldn't really tell if he was angry.

"The door wasn't locked," Shaka said, squaring his shoulders, and meeting his grandfather's eyes. "What you doing home so early?"

"But eh-eh, since when I answer to you, boy?" The man chuckled at the very idea, settling in his chair.

"You lucky is me and not your mother. Lord, looka muddy!" Pappy laughed harder.

"We weren't doing nothing," Shaka said. "Just working on a school project."

"Hey, I believe you," Pappy said.

"Yeah?"

"Yeah. If you all were up to something I'd ah smelled it on you. You all still smell as innocent as morning dew."

She giggled at this in spite of her nervousness. That drew the old man's gaze in her direction. His eyes lingered, and she began to feel uncomfortable.

Then he spoke, "Who's your friend?"

He eased forward as he said this, until he was at the very edge of his chair.

Shaka introduced her but his grandfather didn't seem to be listening; his eyes never left her face, even when she raised her hand to shake his.

"Pappy," Shaka said. And his grandfather seemed to refocus on the conversation. He took her hand and shook it. The twinkle was back in his eye. Inclining his head toward his grandson but not taking his eyes off her, he said, "I hope this one behaving himself."

He settled back in his recliner.

"Yes sir," she replied.

"Pappy," he said, "everybody call me Pappy. You might as well, too."

He was still watching her funny but seemed to have no more to say.

"How come you home so early?" Shaka tried again.

"Slow Monday," Pappy mumbled, lying back in his chair and closing his eyes.

The truth was she was glad for his Pappy's interruption. She wasn't sure about much right now but she was pretty sure she wasn't ready for the other things that could happen being alone in a room, with a boy...and kissing. She hadn't really felt much when they kissed. Maybe a slight dipping and diving in her belly? But she'd felt much more the first time she'd played for him. Playing for him had felt like she was giving him some part of herself that she never showed to anybody. And although she knew that kissing could lead to other things, it wasn't something that pulled at her. She wasn't ready to share her body with him or with anyone. But as much as it scared her to show him her heart through her music, she wanted to share that with him.

Father Ellie was delighted that she was involved in the musical. There was a new message from him every time she logged on, asking how things were going.

She settled in her chair and looked around the computer lab. As usual, no one was studying her. Given where they were a video chat was out of the question, though, so she started to type.

ZGuitarGirl: *Hi, u there?*

Dubliner58: *I'm here. So, how's it going?*

ZGuitarGirl: *K*

Dubliner58: *Just okay?*

ZGuitarGirl: *Think I'm starting 2 get the hang of socialising*

Dubliner58: *See, sometimes you surprise yourself. Glad you went for it.*

ZGuitarGirl: *Didn't really have a choice…*

Dubliner58: *Ah, the boyfriend.*

ZGuitarGirl: *He's not my bf*

Dubliner58: *Okay, okay. The boy who is your friend. What did he do to twist your arm?*

ZGuitarGirl: *He promised to let me help him write a song*

Dubliner58: *Wow, you've come a long way!*

ZGuitarGirl: *Yeh*

Dubliner58: *Well, boyfriend or not, I'm happy for you.*

ZGuitarGirl: *I guess…*

Dubliner58: *Hey, hey, hey, no second guessing!*

ZGuitarGirl: *K*

Now the exchange lagged as she took a few deep breaths and typed quickly before she could stop herself.

ZGuitarGirl: *Father Ellie, u think Im beautiful?*

The question embarrassed her.

Was she being weird? she wondered. She knew the whole situation was weird but he was her mentor and had always been someone she could talk to. Who else was she going to ask? There was a long pause and she cringed, waiting. Finally, his response popped up on the screen.

Dubliner58: *All God's children are beautiful Zahara. Why do you ask?*

ZGuitarGirl: *He said so. Shaka*

Dubliner58: *And you don't believe him?*

ZGuitarGirl: *Jus cuz Im light dont mean Im beautiful*

Dubliner58: *You think the only reason Shaka said that is because of your colour?*

ZGuitarGirl: *Well, no…*

Dubliner58: *Where's all of this coming from?*

ZGuitarGirl: *Doing a school project. On "colourism in the Caribbean"*

Dubliner58: *Ah, the elephant in the room.*

ZGuitarGirl: *?*

Dubliner58: *When I first moved to the Caribbean I assumed everyone was equal. But a lot of people don't see it that way.*

ZGuitarGirl: *Hmm, I should interview u*

Dubliner58: *Or you could crack a book.*

ZGuitarGirl: *Yea. Ive read stuff but its good to get an outside perspective*

Dubliner58: *Well I've been here 30 years now. I don't think I count as an outsider anymore! It's an idea though. How about you do some reading first? I'll send you a list then we can take it from there.*

ZGuitarGirl: *Thanks Father Ellie*

Chapter 10

"Pappy ah blight you, man," Kong joked.

The entire crew was having a good laugh at Shaka's expense. He'd told them the embarrassing story; he told them everything. Well, not quite everything. He hadn't told them how he felt when Zahara played for him and he hadn't told them how relieved he'd felt at the sound of his grandfather's voice.

Almost everyone in the Lion Crew got roles in the production. Mr. Perry had seen their performance at the school fête and had had the bright idea of having them form Anansi's chorus line. So his boys would share his spotlight, doing background dances each time he waltzed Granny away from her ground.

As the programme was a Culture Department production, one of its dance instructors, Mr. Sammy, had been assigned to do the choreography. Mr. Sammy was trained in the Caribbean folk dance tradition. Mr. Perry pressed the choreographer to incorporate the Crew's' more modern moves into the dance numbers.

"They have good ideas, Sammy," Mr. Perry said. "Use them."

Shaka could see that Mr. Sammy wasn't too pleased with Mr. Perry's suggestion; but he was also lazy and they worked that in their favour. Monkey especially appeared to be delighted, because if Shaka was the best dancer, Monkey was the one who could mimic the moves in every music video or musical he saw, adding his own personal twist.

"You could be a choreographer," Mr. Perry commented after observing Monkey demonstrate some moves for Anansi's first act. Monkey ducked his head and hunched his shoulders as though waiting to be teased. But none of the Crew teased him, not even Kong.

Kong was busy learning how to keep time on a djembe drum. He couldn't dance with his bad foot so he'd be drumming, his contribution to the dance. The Crew's drumming and chanting would be the accompaniment for Granny and Anansi during the early parts of their dances. After the chanting and drumming fad-

75

ed, the beat would get hype, the band coming in as the Crew did their dancing thing. For it to work the timing had to be just right, and as the summer wore on the rehearsals, Mr. Perry warned, would get more and more intense.

Because Mr. Perry had them working in groups simultaneously, it was sometimes hard to do the filming for Zahara's school project, harder still to keep track of each other. But they managed.

Zahara was the one filming as Shaka and Nicola, the girl who played Granny, practiced their first dance number.

"Nicola, you need to relax," Mr. Perry said repeatedly to the girl.

Zahara had said she knew her, that she was in one of the upper forms at her school. Shaka had easily assessed that Nicola thought she was miles above him.

"Once the music gets under her skin, Granny is lost. Think of it as a romance," Mr. Perry continued. And Nicola's neck did one of those rolls, a silent *as if*.

Mr. Perry suggested Shaka and Nicola should spend some time getting to know each other. Nicola objected to that.

"He's a low-life," she said. "Granny wouldn't want to spend any time with *him*."

Mr. Perry looked at her. At first she glared back but then, when the teacher didn't back down, Nicola's eyes dropped.

Later, as he reviewed the footage with Zahara, it was obvious that Nicola had scrunched up her nose every time he had so much as breathed near her. Zahara must have seen the same thing.

"She clearly don't like you," she said.

"She's a stuck-up bitch," Accident said as they walked home from practice the next day.

The rehearsal had run longer than usual due to Anansi and Granny's obvious lack of chemistry. Shaka and Nicola had been trying to work on that by spending more time together, but it hadn't done them much good. On stage with Nicola he felt the way they must have looked: as awkward as two toddlers on a play date.

"Can't manufacture chemistry," Kong said, sagely.

"Yes, oh mighty Kong," Shaka said, but without the usual flourish. He laughed but it was half-hearted.

He was thinking about Nicola and how people like her saw people like him. She was *socie*, lived in a wealthy part of the island, and automatically dismissed him as ghetto. She didn't know him. Sure, he lived in a poor neighbourhood, but most people he knew were hard working people, like Pappy driving his taxi and his mother cleaning rooms at a hotel. Nicola, on the other hand, was picked up from rehearsals every day in her lawyer-mother's sleek blue Volvo SUV. He and his Crew weren't less than anybody. But girls like Nicola certainly went out of their way to make them feel that way.

Zahara, he'd realized, was from somewhere in-between. Her Granny had a good job with her public service posting at the Prime Minister's office. She was middle class, her neighbourhood a slight notch up from his, her colouring giving her several legs up in some people's eyes. He was glad that though she seemed aware of her 'status', she didn't buy into it the way girls like Nicola did.

As for Nicola, she was just going to have to get over herself because he wasn't about to let her stuck-up ways spoil their summer production. He was having too much fun.

Shaka wasn't a fan of calypso music; none of them were.

"Calypso is old people music," Accident joked and most of them agreed. He knew you could say the same thing about jazz but at least he found jazz interesting.

Especially like with Ella and Satchmo, when the voice itself became an instrument. Kind of like beatboxing, he'd always thought.

"Well, you used to think Anansi was old-time stories, didn't you?" challenged Mr. Perry. The teacher was pushing them to create a signature calypso rhythm for Granny and Anansi. There was a composer attached to the production, but the director wanted the cast members' input.

Shaka was still trying to warm up to the idea that he could have a say in things. He knew the others were too. The most they could come up with was the remake of King Obstinate's "Shiny Eyes" that Tian Winter did a while ago. Someone suggested the Mac Truck remix of that Swallow song, but then couldn't remember the name. It all sounded so dated to them.

"Nah man Anansi timeless," Dan piped up.

Shaka didn't like to agree with the guy who'd macked on his girl the first time they'd met. Dan the Man, as he and the Crew had taken to calling him, had chilled out since, though, and Shaka had to admit he was right about Anansi.

Mr. Perry said, "Each of you bring me something from the calypso canon that would work for Anansi and Granny."

Dan's new nickname provided inspiration.

Shaka vaguely remembered an old Sparrow song, one Pappy used to like playing. He was digging through the record collection later that afternoon when he heard a noise. He looked up to find Pappy hovering just behind him. He felt like a child caught with his hand in the cookie jar.

"Boy, ent I tell you not to trouble my things when I not here?"

"I looking for a Sparrow song for rehearsal."

"That's not the point. Respect other people's things."

He was surprised at the sharpness of Pappy's tone. Sure, Pappy could be a grump who was particular about his things, but it wasn't the first time he'd dug through his grandfather's music. Granted Pappy usually wasn't around when he did so, unless they were doing it together, but it had never occurred to Shaka that he would have a problem with it.

"Sorry," he mumbled, beginning to put everything away, preparing to close the cabinet.

Pappy's voice stopped him.

"Hmm, you haven't come to me for music in a while, less and less since you start working at that radio station."

His grandfather's voice had softened; now he sounded almost apologetic.

Pappy's comment made him realize that it hadn't even occurred to him to check the station. His hours there had always been irregular, and now that he was seeing Zahara and practicing for the musical, he hadn't gone to the station in a while.

"Move," said Pappy, nudging him with his foot.

He shifted to the side and watched as Pappy pulled out the Sparrow record without even seeming to look for it.

Shaka shook his head.

"When you goin' teach me your system, Pappy?"

"To give you license fu go through me subben an dem?"

His grandfather was putting on his gloves, wiping the vinyl, and settling it in place as he spoke. He signalled Shaka to crank up the phonograph. It was an old, familiar rhythm that felt like home to them both.

Hearing it again, he realized why the calypso "Dan is the Man" had resonated with him as a boy, enough anyway for him to remember. It was all the nursery rhyme stuff like "Wynken Blynken, and Nod" and "Humpty Dumpty." He remembered as a boy, singing the word 'ass' when "Dan the Man" would play. That

81

was his favourite part, and even though it was only talking about donkeys, it used to fill him with a strange sort of delight to say the forbidden word. It was the same way kids had enjoyed singing "For Cup" last Carnival knowing full well that adults wouldn't box them for being rude because it was just a song and songs were harmless, especially at Carnival time when normal rules didn't apply.

Except his grandfather had taught him that words *did* matter and songs were powerful. They could shake up the world like a Muhammad Ali punch.

"James Brown said, 'Say it loud, I'm black and I'm proud' and it electrified a movement," Pappy once told him. "What effect you think songs like "Kick Een She Back Doh" having on young girls, eh? De same young girls you all expect to mek picknee wid someday."

Shaka had been surprised to realize his grandfather actually knew that song, that he knew any modern soca songs. He'd always assumed that music produced after the mid-eighties didn't exist for his grandfather.

Listening to the Sparrow song now that he was older, he understood it to be parody, satire, a mockery of the British colonial education system people like Pappy had grown up with. His grandfather was watching him and must have seen light dawning in his eyes.

"You get it now?" Pappy said.

"I think so," he said nodding.

"The thing the British understood," his grand-father said, "the thing that still licking us to this day, is if you can turn a man mind from himself, you have him… you have him."

That night he wrote a rhyme he called "Fictitious Intent." He worked out a beat for it that looped some of the vintage calypso sound, and even some of Sparrow's voice. He downloaded it to his phone and played it for them at rehearsal the next day, rapping over the recording.

"I've been mind-wiped like Total Recall.
So lost in their game,
Can't see past the caul."

He was tired. He'd worked on the rhyme all night not stopping until the sun's first rays lightened his room. After he rapped for the troupe, he just wanted to crash.

He found himself nodding off as others shared the calypso songs they'd found. By the time it was Zahara's turn to share, he was not only sleepy, he fell asleep sitting up and let out a loud snore. Some laughed. Mr. Perry was not pleased. Zahra was livid.

"That was rude," she said afterwards, brushing right past him as they left rehearsal.

"Me min tired, jack."

She kept on walking. Just a while ago he'd impressed everyone including Mr. Perry with his presentation; now he'd not only lost brownie points with the teacher over the whole snoring thing, he'd also pissed off Zahara. He frowned. Okay, so yeah, he'd actually snored during her presentation. But it wasn't his fault she refused to play the damned guitar like she actually wanted to be heard, was it?

He texted her that night, asked her to meet him under their ficus tree.

She didn't respond, but he went anyway. If his mother or Pappy gave him grief, he'd use working a late shift at the station as an excuse. He just hoped his mother wouldn't check and prayed Zahara would be there. They'd never met in the Gardens at night before. He waited.

Would she come? he wondered. He'd never really seen her angry like that before, wasn't sure if she was the type to hold on to it or let it go. When he heard the squeak of the Garden gate, he stood.

"I'm sorry," was the first thing he said.

She didn't answer.

"Share it with me now, nuh?" he coaxed. He could tell she wanted to, but she just shook her head. Now he was annoyed.

"See? That ah the problem. You must have confidence in what you doing. Me could barely hear you today."

She glared at him. He met her glare head on. If she was going to tell him the truth about his lyrics, she should expect the same from him about her playing. For a long moment they stood at a deadlock, glowering at each other, until finally she slumped.

"I'm afraid," was all she said.

He'd know that all along, but exactly what was she afraid of? That's what he couldn't understand. As if she'd read his mind, she shrugged. This time though, he knew it wasn't because she was choosing not to answer but because she didn't understand it herself. Getting up on stage and performing was second nature to him. Besides, he'd always had his boys at his back; they gave him courage and so he didn't even remember to be afraid. On stage, they were just wilding out together, no different than when they were hanging out.

That gave him an idea.

He asked her to return to the Garden the next night. It took only a little egging on before she agreed.

How far you've come, baby, he thought smiling to himself. He knew better than to say the words out loud though. Instead, as she turned to leave, he called out, "Bring your guitar."

Chapter 11

When she was in primary school, Zahara had had a girl crush on a girl named Lauréna Lee; a girl big in body, personality, and charisma who'd started filling out way before the other girls were even dreaming of training bras.

Lauréna Lee had also been the queen of tall tales. Zahara and her classmates would sop up her stories like bread soaking up gravy. Looking back, Zahara could see how ridiculous they had been.

Was the Queen of England going to come and see them perform the maypole? They didn't know, but Lauréna Lee had said the Queen would show up, so they'd danced their butts off at practice in anticipation.

Were there really scouts from Temple University coming to hear their grade six marching band play their rendition of Short Shirt's "Pledge" at the Independence parade? Probably not; but when they marched across the field at the Antigua Recreation Ground and saluted the Governor General, Lauréna Lee's back straight in spite of the big bass drum she carried, they'd turned it up a notch and lifted their knees that much higher. Come to think of it, it was a blessing that Lauréna Lee had used her powers for good because God knows where she would have led them otherwise.

As a child, she had studied Lauréna Lee trying to figure out how she got them to believe every story that came out of her mouth and follow her lead. Zahara wanted to be like her. Mostly though, she was in awe of her, wondered how anyone could be so bold.

Her classmates had all scattered after grade school, and if Lauréna Lee was still on the island Zahara hadn't seen her in the almost three years since she had traded her blue jumper for a plaid one. But it was Lauréna Lee she'd thought of as she'd fine-tuned a calypso melody for her presentation.

As a starting point, she'd jacked King Obstinate's "Dancing Days" and Short Shirt's "Tourist Leggo," not the actual arrangement but the spirit of them. Both songs were full of unbridled energy. She remembered watching the Party Monarch crowds Carnival after Carnival on TV and the way her idol CP and others commanded and the audience responded. She wanted to be like CP when she said "wave" and the audience waved, said "jump" and the audience obeyed. But that kind of magic was beyond her reach.

Lauréna Lee had it. She remembered the girl holding court, and all the other children rapt. And as she'd strummed her song for the presentation, she'd channelled a bit of Lauréna Lee's *oomph*, just a bit, and let it shoot out through her fingers. What came out had had a cocky sound to it, like calypso with a hard rock edge. Or at least it sounded that way when she played it in her room. When she'd played it at rehearsal, it had fallen flat. She couldn't blame him for nodding off. She was mad at herself really.

"Close your eyes," he said from somewhere in the dark, and she turned around, trying to see him, but it was as if he was hiding from her.

"Where are you?"

"Close your eyes," he repeated.

"What?"

"Close your eyes."

"I'm not…why?"

"Trust me," he said.

She took a deep breath, arms tightening around the guitar she held close to her, and then she closed her eyes.

"Play," he said.

"What?"

"Play," he pressed.

"I… I can't…"

"Yes, you can. Play."

She wanted to stamp her feet. She knew he was just trying to help but didn't like this feeling, like he was playing games with her. She kept her eyes closed even when she felt the sting of tears.

"Play, jack," he urged, his voice gentler this time, coaxing her.

And she breathed and breathed again and lifted the guitar. It was awkward since she didn't have her strap and it kept slipping. Still, lashes wet and tears streaking her face, she strummed, conscious that he was out there in the dark somewhere listening to her. And as she played, something about his presence, the attentiveness and encouragement she felt flowing from him had a calming effect on her. Her strumming grew more assured, as if she had the Lauréna Lee *oomph* right there at the tips of her fingers. At the last lick of her pick, she opened her watery eyes to find his face inches from hers. She hadn't heard or felt him come closer. Thinking he might kiss her then, she held her breath; but he merely smiled.

"How you feel?"

She searched her heart.

"Happy," she said.

Her fingers were still tingling, and the electricity of it travelled up the rest of her body until she felt like she had to move, or scratch, or dance, or something. She leaned forward and kissed him. And just like that the spell was broken.

"Woohooo!" a voice hollered.

"Mi boy goin' get some," said another.

And she looked past him, squinting in the darkness, to see Kong, Accident and the rest of them. Shaka rolled his eyes and she tried to be angry but she was still tingling. Besides, of course he'd brought his crew. She knew by now that they were a big part of his life. She kind of envied them that.

"You good, sistren, you real good," Kong said. The others nodded.

91

She blushed. She'd spent a lot of time perfecting her playing, filling up her lonely hours with music; still, she didn't think she was *that* good. But there they were grinning at her, all white teeth in the dark, as though she was something special.

At the next practice, Kong insisted that Mr. Perry and the music director, Ms. Jean, listen to her music again. Mr. Perry was glad to see them taking initiative and was only too happy to indulge.

She took a deep breath, closed her eyes, and played holding nothing back. And the music, and the applause that followed, was almost too much to bear.

The entire *Dancing Granny* cast agreed that they'd found their theme music. The excitement was almost enough to distract her from the tender spots that still hurt from the beating Granny Linda had given her when she found her sneaking in after dark.

Life drama and musical breakthroughs aside, she still had a school project to do, so Zahara and the Crew decided to film her having a conversation with Nicola.

The goal was to get Nicola to open up about what she thought of Shaka. Zahara had observed the lingering tension between them as they went over lines together during practice, but at least Nicola wasn't skinning up her face anymore every time he so much as breathed in her direction.

She waited until near the end of rehearsal when Mr. Perry was engrossed in a character study with the actors playing the wife and the mother-in-law. Everyone else was either idling or working out their own sections.

Zahara set down her guitar and walked over to where Nicola, sitting apart from the others, was silently going over her lines. Zahara was surprised at how much, her dislike of Shaka aside, Nicola had embraced the down-to-earth role considering how *science* she seemed, the kind of girl who turned up her nose at everything and acted like she couldn't mash ants. When she sat down, Nicola immediately leaned in the other direction and continued studying her script. Zahara couldn't help a little smile at the other girl's antics, as she observed Kong, not far away already recording them. She set her own phone to record for backup on sound.

"You're really good," she said.

Nicola didn't answer, just looked at her out of the corner of her eye. She seemed unsure, like she thought Zahara was making fun of her or something.

"I mean it," Zahara went on before she lost her nerve. "You're really good…you even worked the chemistry thing out with Shaka."

Nicola twisted her lips.

"He's alright, I guess."

"Yeah, he is."

Nicola turned to her fully then, as though something had pinged her radar.

"You checking for him?"

Zahara blinked.

"Yeah, I guess I am," she admitted.

Nicola was silent, then her eyebrows slowly lifted and a smirk spread across her lips.

"So, you're a girl after all, I was beginning to wonder about you."

"Wonder about me?"

"Wonder if you were playing for the other side."

"The other side?"

Nicola rolled her eyes like she was slow, then wiggled her hand like Red Foxx on the re-runs of *Sanford and Son* Granny Linda liked to watch.

Zahara blushed and shook her head when she realized what Nicola was talking about.

"No, I'm not into that…men, I mean boys…I like boys…"

94

"You like a *particular* boy," the other girl teased.

The conversation felt so weird, almost like they were girlfriends.

"He's alright I guess," Nicola repeated. They gazed across the room at Shaka. Right then he was forming the fool, walking on his hands across the floor. "Once you get past ...," Nicola began and then her voice trailed off.

"Get past...?"

But Nicola didn't have anything more to say on that subject it seemed. Zahara decided to give her a little push.

"What you mean, 'cause he's dark skinned?"

Nicola laughed.

"Now that's an understatement. He's blacker than an APUA blackout... during a quarter moon...at midnight."

She had thought this was coming, but now that Nicola had actually come right out and said it, she couldn't believe it. She didn't know what to say.

"What?" Nicola said defensively. "I said he was alright. Plus, he got that good hair, kinda like yours."

The strange thing was that Nicola was darkskinned too. Not as dark as Shaka, but not light either. And it wasn't like skin colour was any measure of beau-

95

ty, no matter what people like Nicola and Dan the Man thought. After all, s*he* was light-skinned yet Nicola definitely had her beat in the looks department.

Looking at her up close, she could see how unblemished Nicola's skin was, smooth and even-toned, compared to her own, now patterned with summer heats. Nicola had one of those standard cover-girl faces: cheekbones for days, nose, lips, and perfectly-shaped eyebrows positioned just so, and a cute pixie cut to top it all off. Her clothing and accessories looked expensive and she somehow managed to always look fresh and put-together, even after hours of practice, when the rest of them looked dishevelled and tired.

Girls like Nicola made Zahara feel almost oafish by comparison. They had the kind of sparkling finish that made it seem like they had primped and prepped for hours, and yet never seemed like they were trying too hard.

Yet the way Nicola talked about colour made Zahara wonder what was behind all that style and sophistication. *Did Nicola see herself as beautiful? Or did Nicola put on airs because deep down inside she was afraid she wasn't?*

Later, alone in her room, Zahara found herself thinking about the power of the 'but' as she read one of the books Father Ellie had suggested. She'd been able to find most of them in the library. Nicola's comment about 'good hair' had even prompted her to pick up a copy of Althea Prince's *Politics of Black Women's Hair*.

She thought about what Shaka had said when they'd listened to the audio of her conversation with Nicola.

"What? You think me don't know me black?" he'd laughed. Then he'd leaned in to steal a quick kiss and added jokingly, "But me cute though, right?"

Black but cute. Nicola had said as much. It was a modifier; she knew that much about grammar. As if the word 'black' needed dressing up or dressing down, changing, before it could be granted the right to exist. As if 'black' didn't have a right to just be. It bugged her that something that really shouldn't matter, mattered so much.

Her grandmother had found her staring at herself in the mirror more times than she cared to recall. She knew Granny Linda thought she was becoming vain. And she really *was* taking more care with her hair, although she didn't feel there was much she could do with a giant afro puff aside from changing up the ribbons pulling it together. She'd also started adding a trace of gloss to her lips, but that was mostly because Shaka liked the cherry flavour when they kissed. He would lick his lips and whisper how sweet she tasted, though it felt like a lie because it wasn't really her now was it? She wasn't thinking about those things when she gazed in the mirror tonight though. She was just trying to unravel the mystery of black skin and why it mattered so much.

Chapter 12

Talking about colour...and girls...always made him think of Andra Small, the first girl he'd ever checked for.

They were in grade six when suddenly Andra had grown these twin peaks on her chest. Andra, the best athlete in school, who'd always been like one of the boys, was suddenly a girl. Weird.

He'd felt bad for her when some of the guys started calling her "Big Bubby Small." She'd started keeping to herself, had given up any sport where she had to play on a team. But she'd stuck with her running and continued killing it at cross-country. Even back then, he'd known what was going on, how Andra, once she'd developed, preferred to do things alone. She'd didn't want to stand out in a group of girls; in fact, she'd stopped hanging out with the other girls altogether. Or perhaps more correctly, they'd stopped wanting to hang out with *her*.

One day, they'd been doing laps around the track during PE, everyone except Kong who always got a pass because of his leg. Shaka had spent the time composing a rhyme in his head as he ran, too distracted to notice the burn in his legs. He didn't come back to himself until he'd felt the need for a pen and his notebook to write down the lyrics before they slipped away. That's when he'd realized everyone else was in the middle of the track. His classmates had dropped out one by one and were cheering on the only two runners left on the track: him and Andra Small.

They'd been neck and neck, and he remembered the look of deep concentration on her face. Even now, he wondered what she'd been thinking about. He'd never been particularly athletic. He did what he could for his House on Sports Day, had shot hoops with his boys for as long as he could remember, and rooted for teams during the NBA playoffs. But he'd never cared about being an athlete himself. Andra had obviously cared. She'd pushed herself hard, invested in winning. Not only was he not invested in winning, now that his mind was back in his body he was feeling every burn. He'd caught a stitch and pulled back, and she'd won.

The girls had swarmed around her and from where he'd stood doubled over and panting, he'd seen the look on her face. She was just happy to be one of the girls again. He'd felt good, like he'd given her something she'd been missing. Though it wasn't like he'd let her win; she'd always been the better runner.

His body had hurt for days afterwards and when the track coach had chosen him and Andra for Inter-School games, he'd tried everything he could to get out of it. Thankfully, the boys from the other schools had been more invested and more talented on the track than he was. The best he'd ever pulled off was third place. Endurance running was hard when you were actually in your body to feel the burn.

Andra though, had won her heats and for once everyone had focused on her running and not her chest. She'd also seemed to have gotten that area under control somehow. He figured that someone had recommended sports bras for her. At the time, he'd just been relieved that she'd gotten them to behave. They were distracting. And he'd never liked it when the other boys ogled her.

Andra Small had been his first crush.

They had become friends during the afternoon practices back when he was still prepping for the Inter-School games. He'd walk her as far as the roundabout where they'd break off in opposite directions. With the games over, though, there was no reason to continue that routine. He went back to walking home with the boys, but found he couldn't stop thinking about her. The guys noticed, of course, and teased him about it. He shrugged it off at first. But he'd liked Andra and had a feeling she liked him back. She may have become silent and sullen but she'd always had a smile for him.

When the summer had come and they had gone their separate ways, he'd regretted not acting on the attraction. Next year they'd be in different schools.

He'd decided to check her at home and had taken the boys with him, for company and as backup.

"Man, mi leg ah hat me, all dis walking fu wan gyal," Kong griped, leaning exaggeratedly on the old wooden grandfather cane.

Shaka ignored him. He knew Kong was using the cane to step up his swagger more than anything else. His friend needed the exercise anyway; milking the sore foot for all it was worth was making him lazy.

"Arwe na even know where she lib," said Monkey, who always had to echo Kong.

102

"We'll just go to the playing field," he said for the millionth time. "Somebody there bound to know her. She's an athlete."

"Some people use this thing called phones, you know, maybe you've heard of them?" was Accident's comeback.

It was mutiny. Soon, even Big Head and Scaly would have something to say.

"Yeah, you have one?" Shaka shot back.

It was a low blow. Accident was the poorest among them and didn't have a landline telephone in his house much less a cell phone. Besides, he and Andra had never exchanged numbers; they hadn't had that kind of friendship. Sure, he could've looked her up in the phone book. How many Smalls could there be? But her parents might have answered. So, the trek to the playfield was the best plan. They'd all agreed to it, so he didn't know what they were griping about now anyway. Leave it to Kong to always stir things up.

"We almost reach," Kong said trying to soothe things over as though he hadn't started the whole thing in the first place. When Shaka gave him a look, Kong gave a slight shrug that might have been an apology, not that Kong was the apologizing sort. Kong was giving him a break now, but he knew his friend would never let him forget that he'd been nervous to talk to a girl, and 'Big Bubby Small' of all girls.

At the playfield, there was a scattering of people in the stands. A half-hearted football match was in progress. He had spotted Andra right away standing with a clutch of girls at the far end of the stands, cleaning off their cleats. He didn't know she'd started playing football again. Her jersey was a slightly different colour than the others suggesting that she was the goalkeeper, still effectively a loner. She seemed to fit in okay with these girls though. They were talking loudly and all at once, laughing and pushing at each other.

"Hi, Andra," he said, feeling shy all of a sudden. His boys hung back. None of the girls reacted.

"Andra. Hi," he said louder. She looked up then, her eyes widening. But before she could speak, another of the girls said with a smirk.

"Ah who you?"

And the other voices followed.

"Andra, ah you boyfriend that?"

"Lard, he good black!"

"But he kinda cute though."

Andra continued cleaning her shoes, head bowed, as if he wasn't even there. And he kind of wished he wasn't by that point. He just stood there, skin warm.

"Na bother with dem, bunch ah dutty foot." It was Kong speaking, and he felt his friend's arm around his shoulders, pulling him away. "Come, Zulu."

The girls burst out laughing, all except Andra.

"Ah Zulu fu true."

One of the girls started making jungle sounds, cracking the rest of them up even more. He left the field with his head bowed, feet dragging. His boys were talking too loud, all at once, dissing the girls.

"As if Big Bubby Small all that…she na even all that pretty."

They tried their best to lift his spirits as they made their way out of the playfield.

"You call mi gyal dutty foot," said a boy now blocking their path.

If it had been just him, they might have been able to just push past; but, like Shaka, he had his crew and soon they were brawling. His first fight, only fight to date; after all, they weren't a gang, no matter what some people might think.

"Boss, she ha fu play wid arwe from now on," Monkey said.

"She nah go agree to that."

Ever since they'd heard Zahara play in the Gardens, the Crew had been bugging him to get her to perform with them. It was nearing the end of July, the pre-Carnival fête season, and his boys had got it into their heads that they could land some gigs, maybe even a guest spot on the Teen Splash show, one of the big shows of the season. Shaka knew this was a pipe dream. But try telling his Crew that. They thought they had a real shot at getting booked with Zahara in the group.

But he was trying not to push Zahara too much. She'd told him her Granny had actually given her licks with a belt after catching her sneaking back into the house that night they'd met in the Botanical Gardens. He knew she wasn't ready to take any more risks yet.

Baby steps, he kept reminding himself. Between rehearsals for the musical and the Social Sciences project, there was already a lot going on.

Chapter 13

One of Shaka's boys, Kong, found a video online of a performance entitled *Brown Girl in the Ring*. It was based on an Antiguan poem about the issues Zahara had been exploring. She came over to Shaka's place one day after rehearsal and they watched it together. Well, she watched it, he watched her, saying he'd seen it already.

She was too focussed to let him distract her. This was exactly the kind of thing she'd been looking for.

It opened with young girls, some black, some white, clapping and skipping in a circle, as they sang a rhyme she remembered from her younger days.

'There's a brown girl in the ring, tra la la la la.

And she looks like a sugar and a plum!'

Then a woman, striking with her kinky natural hair and her smooth black skin, stepped out of the circle.

As she did, the singing faded, and the other girls faded with it, into the back ground. This left the woman to command Zahara's attention as she explored in rhythm and verse her bumpy journey to self-love as a dark-skinned black woman in the Caribbean.

It was riveting.

The woman spoke about how a girl could get all turned around in a society that told her she wasn't beautiful because she was black, how that girl might get lost but then find herself by going back to her roots, by coming back to herself, the only person she couldn't really run from in the first place. Zahara kept hitting repeat. This woman was saying everything she wanted to say. On an impulse, she lunged toward where Shaka sat across from her at the edge of his bed, the only space to sit in his room, and hugged him, catching his look of surprise just before he leaned forward, into it, holding on.

"Ah na me, ah Kong," he said, when they broke apart. "This time his search for girls on the Internet actually turn up something useful."

"Pervert," she teased.

"He sure is," he agreed, with that impish glint in his eyes and saucy smirk on his lips that made her want to kiss him.

She turned back to his laptop screen instead, once again mesmerized by the main actress as she boldly claimed her skin, her hair, her heritage.

"She's beautiful," she said. "No *buts* behind her black."

He laughed at that.

"You checking out girls' butts now?" And she smacked him on the arm.

She continued replaying the video, making notes.

"It'd be cool to talk to her," she said after a time.

There was no answer from him. When she looked over he was stretched out, eyes closed, lips moving. *Writing then.* She smiled. She hated to interrupt him, but she was overwhelmed and had to talk to him. She nudged his leg slightly. He "hmmm'd," eyes still closed.

"The woman in the video," she said. "It'd be cool to talk to her, right, I mean she saying exactly what I'm trying to say, right? This better than this, this prettier than that, this hair good, this hair bad, treat people like they matter depending on what shade they are… it's crazy right? Not like we can shed our skin…"

Shaka was upright now and opening his mouth to say something. She knew just what it was too.

"Bleaching doesn't count," she said. And he laughed.

"You ah mind reader now?" he joked.

But she was too wound up about the assignment to be distracted.

"This is serious," she said. "Our history messed us up and we like we don't even know it, walking 'round hating ourselves."

"Sound like you starting to write your paper," he said.

The paper, she thought, *she didn't even know where to start with that.*

She sighed, "It's too much, jack. An identity crisis hundreds of years old. I don't even begin to know how to tackle it. I don't know what Mrs. Keener was thinking. This bigger than us."

She was breathing hard. Then his hands were on her shoulders, squeezing gently.

"Relax."

"But…"

"Relax," he repeated. "Yuh teacher nar ask you fu solve the world problems. She just want to know wha' you ha fu say 'bout this particular problem."

She laughed. "What am I supposed to say? Colourism bad? I think even the people that bleaching know that. They see the social advantage and so they play the game anyway."

"What social advantage," he scoffed. "Smadee jus' ah laugh atta dem."

"Ha! Guys say that, but they always checking for the lightest girl in the room!"

He started rapping then, beating a tattoo on her legs with his fingers.

When had his hands wandered to her legs?

Still rhyming, he obviously wasn't after anything. She started listening, really listening, to what he was saying.

"Don't play the game, it'll drive you insane, thinking you can shed your skin is wishful thinking, but knowing you can shape your mind, that's the real thing…"

It wasn't great but she appreciated that he was trying to distract her *and* help her process everything she'd soaked up these past few weeks and just now in the video, through music. She started humming a melody that rapped itself around his staccato rhythm. They were smiling at each other as they freestyled, improvised, created together.

And as he rhymed and she hummed, she couldn't help thinking that like her melody and his rhythm, they complemented each other. He was so laid back and cool and she was so reserved and tense. She got him

111

caring about the things she cared about; he got her to 'ease up, jack.'

She wondered sometimes if she would have been different, more like him maybe, if her mother hadn't gone out fêting that night, if she hadn't died. In her mind, that's when she became a fretful child and her Granny Linda a sad woman. But she'd still been so young then so what did she know. And, as for the fretting, what had it done but isolate her, keeping her too lost in her head to really connect with others.

Until now. Until Shaka, who helped her clear her mind by rapping with her as she hummed, the two of them riffing off of each other, losing track of time, until his mother came home.

"Time for you to go home, Zahara," his mother said, popping her head around the door she'd told them both must remain open at all times.

Zahara jumped up right away. Shaka's mother didn't fuss about her being around but she was very clear on her rules. Shaka said she had even sat him down for a conversation on not bringing no "chick chick and come come" in her house before he finished school. That conversation had made *both* of them blush even as he re-told it, because they weren't even close to thinking about doing anything that might result in unplanned babies.

Shaka's mother turned now toward her son who was getting up with slower movements, like an old man. And Zahara muffled a smile when he scowled as his mother ordered, "Make sure you walk Zahara to the bus stop, wait with her, and come straight back home, you hear?"

"Me know, me know," he mumbled.

His mother left.

Zahara let her smile out as he grumbled after his mother was out of earshot, "'Make sure you walk Zahara to the bus stop, wait with her, and come straight back home.' That's code for 'don't you dare walk her all the way home and come in my house when night done break.' Tink she slick."

Zahara laughed. For all his chat, Shaka did just as instructed—saw her to the bus stop and on to the bus before turning toward home.

She dreamt about the "Brown Girl" ... and Snow White, and Barbie, and freaking Hannah Montana. Woke up convinced that they were the ones still messing up girls like the one in the video. They were the first idols for young girls like that, girls like her. And who wouldn't want to have their lives? Except for the whole wicked step-mother poisoned apple thing, of course. Oh, and that part where Hannah white-girl-twerked—wining by another name still wining—and stuck her tongue out.

They were rioting in her head, all through her morning routine, all these celeb realities and fairy tale formulas, and she couldn't make any sense of them. Take Beyoncé for example, fem girl icon, superstar, the fiercest. Yet there she was in that one photo wearing the spidery looking crocheted body suit, draped over leopard print fur, and so blonde and airbrushed Zahara didn't recognize her. She'd stared hard, squinted, and, nope, it still looked like someone had put a papier-mâché head on the singer's body. But everybody said Bey was beautiful and she certainly strutted like she thought she was, so was that it? Being beautiful meant not being yourself?

It was all so confusing.

She was still musing over all this and fiddling with her guitar, not really playing, when Shaka texted her the name and number for the woman who had written and acted in the *Brown Girl* YouTube video.

For a moment she just looked at the number then texted him back.

How???

Antigua small, was his only response.

She didn't ask how he knew that she'd wake up obsessing about it.

She also didn't call right away.

"You call yet?" he asked later at rehearsals.

"No," she admitted. He made a grab for her cell.

"I'll do it, I'll do it," she insisted.

He gave her a look that said, "Well, what are you waiting for?"

She stepped out onto the gallery in front of the building and punched in the number. As she waited for an answer, she leaned over the metal rail, eyes fixed on the playing field beyond where some boys were practicing cricket in batting cages made of chicken wire.

"Hi," she said when the woman answered. She was nervous but she tried to speak calmly and slowly. "You don't know me but…"

The lady, Ms. George, was really gracious though. She listened to Zahara's word salad about the video, her school project, all the books she'd been reading, and all the things she'd been thinking, obsessing about, and observing in their interactions in rehearsals and everywhere.

If Ms. George thought it odd that this random girl had tracked her down, she didn't say so.

She laughed warmly and said, "I understand. I'm happy to help."

Ms. George asked Zahara where she'd be the next day noon-ish or even five-ish.

"Probably still at rehearsals," she replied. And the woman chuckled at that.

"The director pushing you all hard, eh; I know a little something 'bout that. Tell you what. I'll come by there. Where are the rehearsals?"

She was even more beautiful in person.

"The bottom line," she said, "is self-love no matter what colour, shape, or size you are. If you don't love yourself, who goin' love you?" she asked. "No other race of people has to work so hard to know their worth because no other race of people had it so beaten out of them, so beaten we can't even see what we doing to ourselves.

"Love yourself," she said. "Dig deep for the things that reflect you, and if it not there, you make it. You're part of this too."

Just before she left, the poetess gave Zahara a copy of Poems by Maya Angelou. She told her to read "Phenomenal Woman" in her room by herself.

"Say the words out loud," she said. "And mean them."

After that, she was gone, like some kind of guardian angel from a dream, like Frankie Avalon singing to Frenchie in the dream sequence from *Grease*.

"So?" Shaka asked when they were walking home after rehearsals. She held the Maya Angelou book in her hand.

"So," Zahara replied. "She's cool."

Chapter 14

Mosquitos aside, it was nice out. Fresh smelling like after a shower indicating it had rained earlier while they'd been in practice. Not too many stars but a cool breeze and pleasant night sounds. Not gun shots and arguments, but a choir of crickets and Cuban frogs harmonizing while a dog barked a solo; now and then a car going by added a little exclamation point.

Home by dark didn't have to mean inside by dark, the way he saw it, at least not until he was called in, so he stayed put on the front porch after his boys had shoved off to their own homes. He could live with the mosquitos for a few more minutes.

He felt happy. Pappy's TV, the news on low volume so he could say he watched it even if he wasn't really paying attention; footsteps in the front bedroom, his mother shedding her work clothes before finishing up the dinner chores he'd started earlier was a part of that feeling. He didn't examine it too closely but the rhythm of their evenings, all of them present and accounted for, made him feel comforted, safe.

Tonight his girl was on his mind more than anything. He'd loved, loved, loved being able to put a smile on her face especially after she'd managed to stress herself out, over something her classmates probably weren't even bothering to do. He liked that she cared so much, hated that she worried so much, loved that he could make her smile. Could feel his own face stretch into a responding smile, though he was sitting on his porch in the semi-dark and she was nowhere around.

He didn't even mind having to give credit to Kong, if only in his mind. It was Kong who, when he'd said earlier, "I wish Z could talk to the woman in that video for real," had replied "Why can't she?"

When he'd stated the obvious, that they didn't have the woman's number, Kong had rolled his eyes, "Boss, the woman name right dey pon the video."

When he still didn't see how that gave him her number, Kong had simply strolled into his house and into his room like he owned the place, powered up his computer, and with just a few clicks pulled up the woman's number.

The beginning of a rhyme—"unearthing secrets like Snowden"—popped into his head making his fingers itch to grab a pen and write it down, at the ease with which his friend tracked down the lady. It was like the age of the Terminator. And that analogy sent his mind on another lyrical tangent so that his friend had to cuff him to get his attention. They'd scuffled after that, of course. He'd briefly hesitated, wondering if it wouldn't be weird for them to call the woman when they didn't even know her, prompting Kong cuff him again. Finally, he'd texted Zahara the number.

By the time they'd met up at practice that afternoon though she hadn't even called. At first he thought he'd misjudged but when he realized it was just nerves, he'd waited for her to work up to it, ready to give a little nudge if needed. Seriously it was just another human being, not Khaleesi or Storm or something. When he'd seen the smile on her face afterward, he'd given himself a little mental pat on the back—*who was the best boyfriend evah!?*

He twirled his phone between his fingers, resisting the urge, now that she was occupying his thoughts, to call or text her or something. He'd seen her not an hour ago at practice. In his mind, he heard Kong crack a whip and he smiled self-deprecatingly though no one was around to mock him.

His Crew would tease him if they knew how hooked he was especially considering how PG-rated his relationship with Zahara had been to date. He wasn't complaining. He was cool with it. Making her happy made him happy, and, skittish as she was, he wasn't about to do anything to run her off. Not that he had a clue what that would be exactly, but, yeah, he wasn't about to admit his ignorance on that subject outside of the metaphors and fictions he crafted, not even to himself. The ability to play with words and rhythms was always there, and he was grateful for that.

He was on a roll with it lately too, both the rhyming and the music. The music was proving to be a revelation. Ever since the Sparrow song, he'd returned to drink deep time and again from the calypso well, finding he liked the lyrical depth and the challenge of freshening up the old sounds with more modern rhythms. Ever since yesterday, when she'd been watching the tape, he'd had this old Short Shirt tune, Afro-Antiguan, on loop in his head, the melody every now and again catching on a rhyme, prompting him to reach for a notebook or his recorder.

121

He could even see the notes if he got into the zone. He couldn't read music per se but when he looked up, like now, at the blanketing darkness, in the absence of the stars, he saw squiggly lines in motion, letters dancing around them, loose and fluid like in alphabet soup.

His stomach picked that moment to grumble a reminder about its deprived state and he chuckled.

"Only crazy people si'dung ah laugh to themselves like fool," Pappy teased from the doorway.

He hadn't even heard his grandfather get up from his chair, much less hear the door open. When he looked down from the sky and swung around toward the doorway, he couldn't so much see Pappy's face, backlit as he was by the houselights, as see the glint of his grinning teeth.

"Ah nuh jack-o-lantern me be nuh, wha you ah watch me so like you lost?" Pappy said.

His grandfather didn't wait for an answer, just turned away calling over his shoulder, "Dinner ready."

His stomach rumbled again, in approval, as he went inside and closed the door.

Chapter 15

She didn't quite know how it happened, but she and Nicola had started hanging out together at rehearsals. She wondered if it would spill over into the new school year, when Nicola was in fifth form and she was in third, or if it was some weird summertime fling. She didn't seek out the friendship; that was all on Nicola. Suddenly the former Ice Queen wanted to hang out with the band. She was surprised when Nicola asked her to run lines with her during their breaks.

"Shouldn't you be doing this with Shaka?" she asked the first time.

"I don't know," Nicola teased. "I hear his girl-friend's kind of jealous."

She was even more surprised to hear herself laugh.

Shaka had glanced over at them, his eyebrows shooting up to his hairline when he saw them together. She'd shrugged and tried to send him a look that said, "I'll tell you later", and he'd turned back to practicing his dance moves for Anansi's solo.

The solo was a spider-like dance inspired by moves Monkey had seen a Dutch dancer do on You-Tube. It was proving challenging for Shaka, more like ballet than hip hop or dance hall, way outside of his comfort zone. Surprisingly, Mr. Sammy liked it. The choreographer had been working with the Crew on incorporating some signature Caribbean folk dance moves that would make for a really interesting mix. If Shaka could pull it off.

Zahara knew he was nervous and didn't want to distract him. She silently signalled to Nicola, inviting her outside, and there, sitting on the ground with their backs against the metal rail, they didn't so much run lines as talk about boys. It turned out Nicola had a thing for Dan.

"I used to think you liked him," Nicola confessed. A mischievous gleam entered her eyes. "But now I know you prefer the taste of dark chocolate."

Zahara blushed. Nicola cackled, drawing more attention and causing Zahara to blush even harder.

"Mind your face don't catch fire," the older girl teased. "So, what's he like?"

"Shaka?"

"No, do-do head. Dan."

Zahara's knee-jerk reaction was to tell Nicola how annoying she found Dan, but she held her tongue. The drummer, she'd learned, was very talented but he knew it and wanted everyone else to know it too. She could see how some girls might like him though. His confidence, even if it was actually nothing more than bravado, could be kind of appealing she supposed. And musicians were definitely sexy if the exploits of rock stars were to be believed. Still, Dan the Man?

She cleared her throat, tried to think of something positive to say.

"He's a talented drummer," she said, truthfully.

Nicola nodded. "And sexy, right?"

Zahara tried to smile but just ended up making a face. Nicola was too busy mooning over Dan to notice.

Later she found herself thinking about the whole Nicola and Dan thing. Ever since he'd hit on her that first day of rehearsal, she'd found Dan to be annoying but harmless, like a mosquito that buzzes but doesn't bite. He had opinions on everything and was deluded enough to think everyone wanted to hear them.

It had been easy enough to get him on camera talking about his views on Antiguan girls who apparently were "too nuff" and not pretty on account of being "too black." He actually went so far as to lament the fact that Antiguan girls weren't mixed like the Trini and Dominican girls who he clearly thought were generally prettier.

He'd once asked her if she had some Indian in her, which she didn't, as though he thought it was a compliment.

Did he think he was cute? she wondered.

He was brown, a similar shade to her actually, and had this Caribbean hipster vibe about him–nerdy glasses, roped hair, fuzz coming in on his face. He liked to wear plaid, old-school pants and artsy t-shirts. Okay, she kind of liked the shirts, if not the way they stretched across his soft though not fat belly as if he couldn't be bothered with trying to look cool, and that's what made him cool. She could see him thinking like that.

He was so full of himself and so oblivious to how his views stunk up the place. She couldn't imagine anyone who'd spent more than a second with him being attracted to him. But apparently, Nicola was. She wondered how much of Nicola's attraction to Dan had to do with the fact that he was light-skinned and they were both well-off. After that conversation, she found herself studying Nicola every now and then, wondering if she was, in fact, that shallow. She knew Nicola was studying her too.

Mr. Perry informed them that they'd be previewing part of the musical during the Teen Splash show.

"As a way of promoting the production," he said. "Now is the time to get people psyched up for when we debut later in the summer."

Zahara's heart started hammering. *Would Mr. Perry ask her to play at the preview?* Teen Splash was less than a week away.

"For the preview, we'll give them a peek at the Li-on Crew's skills, just the dancers and the djembe drum," Mr. Perry continued, and she breathed again. "Shaka, we'll use that mix you did for the calypso presentation, and we'll also do a bit of Anansi's solo with the backing dancers."

Zahara wondered if Nicola was mad that she wasn't a part of the preview. The last time they'd run lines together, Nicola had confessed that Teen Splash was her favourite Carnival show, that she'd always dreamed of representing her school in the competition. Nicola was so in love with the show, she could remember in detail her favourite performances from previous years, even some older ones that her mom had copied for her from VHS because she knew she liked the show so much.

"You have to come watch them some time," she'd once gushed to Zahara, though the way Nicola talked about the many girls over the years—the girl, who'd danced to "And the Lord Said;" the one with the guitar who did "On Broadway;" the girl in suit and top hat who tapped like Bill "Bojangles" Robinson; the one who danced on stilts like a moko jumbie to Burning Flames' "We Love to Play Mas;" the girl who'd come out dressed in a huge dashiki and, rocking an even huger afro, to sing the "Negro Anthem"—she felt like she'd seen them all already. Nicola had even confided in Zahara her secret dream of representing their school in the Teen Splash pageant.

She'd asked Nicola why, with only one year left in high school, she hadn't tried out for Teen Splash as yet. And Nicola had shocked her with the confession that she didn't think she was good enough. She could relate to that feeling of course. But Nicola clearly had talent and looks; it wasn't like *she* was a wallflower.

Or maybe wallflowers weren't the only ones who felt insecure? Maybe the showy ones were insecure too? Who would have guessed Nicola had insecurities padlocked behind all of her awesomeness and poise? It just went to show, you never knew with people.

She found herself hoping that Nicola *would* go for it next year. Maybe after the production was done she'd see how special she was, because whatever the other issues with her performance, Nicola could sing and act like Jennifer Hudson in *Dreamgirls*; she was that good. Even the Lion Crew thought so even though they still didn't like her.

But she was slowly starting to understand Nicola. They were forging a kind of stilted friendship. As rehearsal broke up, Nicola nudged her, grinning.

"So we goin' to the Talented Teen together, right? I'll pick you up. Think Dan will come?"

Granny Linda said no.

She'd worked her way up to asking while they were doing laundry; lugging baths of wet clothes from the machine, through the living room, to the clothes line out back, then bringing the dry clothes in to be folded.

They sat on her grandmother's bed, folding as the announcers on Granny Linda's favourite talk radio station reported on the Carnival opening parade, her grandmother tsk-tsking mildly at the behaviour of the t-shirt mas revellers as though she could actually see them through the radio.

It was probably not the best time to ask.

"The production will be doing a preview during the Teen Splash," she began.

"Oh, are you in it?"

It would have been so easy to lie, a simple "yes" and that would have been the end of it. But things had been so tense between them since her last punishment, the night she'd been caught sneaking in, she didn't want to push it. Besides she was just a bad liar.

"No," she said.

Granny Linda continued folding, as though the discussion had ended.

"I want to go though," Zahara said.

"You have to help or something?"

Another opening.

"No," she said.

Another missed opportunity.

"Then you don't need to be a part of that."

"There's nothing wrong with Carnival," she tried. She paused. "Mom loved Carnival." The standards and headpieces in the small room at the back of the house, the one where the guitar had once stood, were evidence of that. Seems like she had vague, very vague memories of glitter on her mother's skin, of her face shining with sweat and laughter, of feathers tickling her face when her mother swept her up into her arms, of her Granny Linda tut-tutting that they'd "be walking naked next."

"Don't talk about things you don't know 'bout," Granny Linda said.

It was a misfire bringing up her mother. Talking about her mother always made her grandmother moody. It wasn't a conversation they had often but Zahara could usually tell when the memories crept up on her. It was so unfair. What was it Father Ellie had said? The elephant in the room?

"I want to go," she pressed.

"No," her Granny replied before the words were even fully out of her mouth.

"Why not?" Zahara demanded, raising her voice.

She knew her words would be seen as backchat. The thing about Granny Linda, by her own mouth, was that she didn't "abide rudeness." Granny Linda didn't see her as a problem teen, and she even suspected that her grandmother might know in her heart of hearts that she deserved a little more rope. Yet Granny Linda would always come down on a direct challenge like a ton of bricks.

So she wasn't that surprised when her grandmother launched at her. She found herself pressed face down into the pile of clothes that quickly scattered over the bed as though they were making a break for it. Granny Linda's hands were still strong and they pounded on her back. She went lax right away, didn't cry or beg, just waited it out. And like a freak storm, it quickly passed.

It was so unfair! She hadn't done anything wrong. And she knew her grandmother knew it too, could tell from the way she tiptoed around her the rest of the day and into the next day that Granny Linda had scared herself with her anger as surely as Zahara had surprised herself with her defiance. It wasn't anything overt like extra food, or, heaven forbid, permission to actually go to the show, so maybe she was just seeing what she wanted to see; but she could tell that her grandmother wanted to say something, maybe apologize. Only she didn't seem to have the have the words.

The Teen Splash show was the next night. She heard Nicola's mother's car horn blow outside. She hadn't said anything at rehearsals that day and now she peeped through the living room window too embarrassed to even go out to the car to try to explain to her new, socially savvy friend that she didn't have permission to go. Nicola didn't even seem like she had to ask to go anywhere, and certainly never seemed to give any consideration to whether or not her mother or father would be free to take her wherever she wanted to go. Their lives couldn't have been more different. The shame she felt, as she called out that she wouldn't be going after all, drove it home for her.

She couldn't see Nicola's face in the dark but she heard the *choops*.

"You couldn't tell me that before you make me come all the way ya?" Nicola demanded.

She didn't have a good answer for that. She heard another loud *choops* from the interior of the car before it drove off.

She went to bed right away but could hear Granny Linda listening to the talking heads give inane commentary during the live broadcast of the Teen Splash on the radio she kept in her bedroom. She was such a hypocrite. If Carnival was so immoral, why didn't she turn off her precious radio during the coverage? Wrapped up in her resentment, Zahara listened to the entire thing from her bed. She heard Shaka's mix when Lion Crew performed, heard the way the crowd roared, heard the announcer whistle appreciatively and say "well that woke everybody up" afterwards. That triggered another round of quiet tears at the unfairness that was her life.

Missed you tnite, he texted.

She didn't text back.

Chapter 16

"Wha' me tell you! Wha' me tell you, boss!" Kong said.

"Stop crowing, man. Me go ha fu start call you 'Rooster' soon," he said, still fiddling with his phone as if it was broken, as if that's why she hadn't texted back.

"Na try to bring me down 'cause yuh gyal na come. Dat was hype no wah!"

"No thanks to you," Big Head teased.

"Shut up," Kong said. "My drumming was bad."

"Yeah, good an' bad," Big Head agreed mockingly. Kong's hand came up to smack the side of his head, but Big Head ducked.

They were all on a high. He'd nailed the spider dance, every crouch and sideways crawl, leap, and pirouette…yes, he'd pirouetted. And when the Crew had emerged from the shadows, the crowd had gone crazy.

Kong's drumming had built the atmosphere; all jokes aside he was getting good on those things. Then when Shaka's own music mix had kicked in, the crowd had gone crazy like Tian Winter was on stage or something. They'd broken the hip-hop mould and given the crowd everything from salsa and calypso to folk dance fusion.

The only thing missing had been Zahara. She hadn't been there to witness it and now she wasn't answering her phone.

"Wha' happen to you last night?" he asked as soon as he saw her enter the rehearsal hall the next day.

"Why everybody keep asking me that?" Zahara looked irritated, and from the cold shoulder he'd seen Nicola give her over by the door, it looked like she and Ms. Socie were back to not talking. He'd be lying if he said he cared about that right now.

Zahara was his girlfriend. It wasn't unreasonable for him to want her to come to the Teen Splash to see him dance, his first time dancing on a stage that big, before so many people. Pappy and his mom hadn't been there, but they'd watched it on television and had both stayed up to congratulate him when he got home. He'd felt like a celebrity. He didn't need his own girl bringing him down. Sometimes, he wished she wasn't so high maintenance.

"I thought you'd be there," he said.

"Well, you thought wrong."

Just that, no explanation. At that he'd had enough. He turned away with a *choops* heard all around the room.

He was muttering to himself as he made his way back over to his boys.

"Hey, forget she man…" Big Head started to say.

"Na talk 'bout she," he snarled. "None ah-you ha nothing fu say 'bout she."

He stalked out of the building, slamming the door behind him. He was pacing on the gallery when Mr. Perry came out.

"You did good last night," Mr. Perry said.

Shaka only grunted. He didn't stop pacing.

Mr. Perry held his arm to still him and he tried to pull away, but while Mr. Perry was a clean cut, compact man with his long-sleeved buttoned-down shirts, pressed jeans, and thin framed glasses, he had steel in his grip. Unable to shake him, Shaka threw a punch at Mr. Perry, who easily ducked.

But the punch achieved the desired result, Mr. Perry let him go.

Shaka breathed hard, waiting for his punishment. Swinging on teachers, even outside of school, had to be an unforgiveable offence. Instead Mr. Perry smirked.

"That's how you throw a punch?"

"Wha…?"

"That was weak." And the teacher laughed at him.

He felt like he'd just woken up from the Matrix or something, or taken a trip to the Twilight Zone.

"First of all." Mr. Perry came closer, circling him. "Your stance is all wrong."

Shaka just stood there.

"Well, don't just stand there. Come on, left foot forward, right foot back," Mr. Perry said, kicking at his feet until, confused, he assumed the desired stance.

"Right toes out, dip your knees a little bit."

Stunned, he did just that.

Mr. Perry came around to stand in front of him.

"Okay, good." The teacher faced him, his stance similar but steadier. He raised his arms up.

Shaka was amazed. *Were they actually going to fight?*

"Jab like this with your left. Swing right, jab left again. Left, right, left, got it?" Mr. Perry demonstrated the swings as he said this. Still confused about what was going on, Shaka mirrored the moves.

138

"Swivel, turn at the hip with each swing, so that you're not just pushing out with your hands but with your whole torso. Put some power behind it...not so wide, keep your elbows in, nice and tight...that's right...keep your fists up...protect your chin, you don't want me to..."

And Mr. Perry clipped him on his chin, pushing him off balance. With that, his anger flared up again, and he struck out, but with more control this time.

"That's right." Mr. Perry seemed pleased. Shaka was confused again. *Shouldn't he be angry?*

Mr. Perry held up his right arm about chest level, palm first.

"Now, hit my palm."

Shaka swung but only hit air. He struck out again, and again, and again, until he was sweating, but he didn't connect once.

"You keep moving," he complained.

Mr. Perry laughed. "And you think the person you fighting goin' stand there saying, 'Hit me please?' They'd have to be an ass...or a masochist."

A maso-*what?* His brow furrowed.

"Word of the day," the teacher said. It was something he did in English class all the time. Whenever they were confused by a word he used, he'd sing out

139

"Word of the day" and they'd have to write it down, look it up, and come to the next class prepared to use it in a sentence. It was irritating but it had made his essays better.

He supposed Mr. Perry wasn't so bad after all. He'd swung at the man, swung at a teacher, and instead of getting angry, here he was teaching him to box.

It was kind of funny actually.

Shaka stopped trying to hit Mr. Perry, breathing hard, this time from exertion.

"So you're a boxing instructor too?" he asked.

"Not exactly, but I know my way around a punching bag. Better than *being* a punching bag." Mr. Perry chuckled again and put a hand on Shaka's shoulder. "Good way to work off a fit of temper too. So what's got you so wound up?"

He shrugged.

"Is it Zahara?"

He didn't deny it.

"You're mad she wasn't there last night."

He wanted to lie and say he didn't care, but he didn't have the energy. Besides, it kind of felt good to know Mr. Perry cared.

"You have to remember she doesn't rule herself," Mr. Perry said.

"And consider that maybe Zahara's as mad as you that she couldn't be there."

"Hmmm," he mumbled. He guessed that could be it but what was he supposed to do about that?

"Just give her some space."

Mind reader.

"No, I'm not a mind reader," the teacher continued. "But you do realize that you wear every thought on your face?"

He laughed, embarrassed and somehow, lighter. Mr. Perry squeezed his shoulder.

"Now go wash your face and meet us back inside. Don't think 'cause you're a celebrity now you don't have to practice."

"Never," Shaka said with a chuckle, before going off to do as instructed.

Chapter 17

Mr. Perry came over to the band when he came back inside. Shaka wasn't with him. She wanted to ask if he'd been sent home or something, but didn't.

"How's that interlude coming along, guys?" he asked, looking straight at her. "Everything okay?"

"We working it out," Dan piped up. Mr. Perry glanced at him but said nothing. His eyes remained focused on Zahara.

"Everything okay, Zahara?" he asked.

She nodded, wondering why he was singling her out. Mr. Perry squeezed her shoulder before turning back to the main part of the rehearsal, Granny's monologue. Her eyes tracked him as he walked up to Nicola, who'd been waiting with increasing impatience, but she wasn't really paying attention as he began guiding her sort-of-friend through the scene. *What had happened with him and Shaka? Why was he asking her if she was okay?*

Dan shuffled closer, cleared his throat.

"So, about Nicola," he said, also staring in Nicola and Mr. Perry's direction. "She looked kinda hot last night. You know if she seeing anyone?"

Zahara rolled her eyes and picked up her guitar. Well, it seemed 'Granny' had finally managed to get the drummer's attention. Perhaps *that* news might get her back in Nicola's good graces.

Whatever his other flaws, Dan was a hell of a drummer, a bit showy with the stick-twirling—a trick he hadn't quite mastered—but also fun to play with.

The other member of the band was an Asian dude with hair styled in a pompadour that Zahara longed to poke to see if it was as stiff as it looked. He'd been christened 'Call Me Ted' by Kong, because that's what he'd said during introductions on the first day, 'Call me Ted,' as though 'Ted' wasn't really his name. Call Me Ted was the cool silent type. He was one of the oldest in the troupe and had already started producing tracks for up-and-coming artistes, which made him infinitely cooler than the rest of them.

Dan the Man and Call Me Ted were always bouncing ideas off of each other. They did this without the need for too many words.

"Check this out," Ted would say pushing a button on the synthesizer.

"How 'bout this?" Dan would respond tapping off a lick on the drums.

Slowly but surely, and with Shaka's encouragement, Zahara was learning to speak up as well.

"So, I have this idea for Granny and Anansi's last dance," she said.

They looked at her expectantly. So she closed her eyes, took a moment to collect herself, and began picking the guitar strings with her fingers, something she never did. Usually she strummed with the pick, making it easier for her to blend into the background. Finger-picking individual strings causing them to screech or sigh, drawing them out or cutting them off as she desired was the 'hey-look-at-me' style of playing she'd usually shied away from. But now she was doing it. It was all coming together; what she'd learned from Father Ellie, what she was still learning from her current music teacher, Mr. Patrick, and what she was discovering for herself.

There was a thin sheet of sweat over her entire body, even her scalp, when she stopped.

"Impressive!" Dan said, his brevity as much of a surprise as his approval.

Call Me Ted nodded. "Good."

They spent the rest of the session knitting the whole thing together. Playing with other instruments was like weaving different coloured threads into a unique pattern. *Yeah, it was fun.*

"Good session today," Shaka said later as they walked home with his crew, the both of them trailing a few paces behind.

"I owe you," she said quietly She knew she'd been unfair to him earlier.

"No, ah you that!"

"Still," she insisted. "I owe you."

"Sorry 'bout earlier," he said, and his voice was softer now.

"Me too. I wanted to come, you know."

"Yeah, me know."

She decided she was going to the Party Monarch that Saturday. Nicola helped her plan how once she explained how strict her Granny Linda was and she hadn't just blown her off, and once she passed on the gossip that Dan had been checking Nicola out.

145

Nicola got her mom to call Granny Linda. She wasn't quite sure what Nicola's mom said. All she could hear was Granny Linda's half of the conversation, mostly "Hmm" and "Mmm-hmm", but when her grandmother hung up the phone she said, "Just make sure you reach in this house before I go to sleep."

That wouldn't be hard to do; Zahara knew Granny Linda wouldn't go to sleep until she got home anyway.

Granny Linda, whether due to guilt or thanks to Nicola's mom negotiating skills, had even agreed to let her go directly to Nicola's house after practice on the day of the Party Monarch. It was a huge leap of faith considering that whenever she left the house Granny Linda liked to check that she was dressed appropriately and felt it necessary to talk her ear off making sure she remembered what was expected of her. As if she could forget after hearing it over and over again.

Nicola was wearing a white short-sleeved body suit with silver panels down the sides and at the neck like a choker with cut-off white jean shorts with frayed edges. She'd spray-painted her shoes silver. Zahara wore a sun-yellow crop top and a pair of jean shorts. She'd packed one of her maxi dresses but Nicola had urged her to borrow something from her closet.

"You don't hear what it's called? Party Monarch. Is not church we going," Nicola teased.

Zahara looked at herself in the mirror, observing her pale legs, her belly button—parts of her that were usually covered up.

"I don't know," she said slowly. Nicola grabbed her arms and turned her away from the mirror.

"Well I do. You look hot. Now for some makeup."

Nicola sat her down and put so much paint on her face, she barely recognized herself. A pair of drop earrings—also Nicola's—finished the look. She felt like a character on *What Not to Wear*. She'd always thought that the people who got makeovers on that show didn't look like themselves afterwards. Nicola rubbed some kind of cream into her hair and pulled her fingers through it trying to unsnarl the kinks. Zahara cringed and winced and Nicola eased up a little.

"I thought you had that good hair," she joked, "but this rougher than mine."

Nicola's hair was straightened so Zahara knew she must mean her natural hair.

Earlier while wandering around the house, she'd seen pictures of Nicola pre-straightening, cute pictures of her with her natural hair parted and decorated with bubbles and ribbons. It was a big house; easily three times the size of her own. There was expensive art on the walls, a game room and a family room, a dining room and a kitchen, and more bathrooms than people. A spiral staircase cut into the middle, effectively dividing the house into two wings. An only child in her own wing, it felt like Nicola lived apart from her parents in her own apartment, an apartment with a raised balcony that had a view of the sea. Sure, Antigua had 365 beaches, but she didn't know anyone with their own personal sea view. That was the house's name, by the way, Sea View, cut into the electronic metal gate at their upward sloping driveway entrance. *Who named their houses apart from people in Hollywood or people who wanted to pretend to be like them?*

She had to imagine that with all this opulence they could afford to have a driver pick Nicola up until it was time for her to get her own car. It would certainly have been easier. But Nicola's mother seemed to enjoy the mother-daughter time that chauffeuring allowed, even if Nicola largely ignored her on the drives. She'd personally witnessed Nicola's mother pressing for details on her daughter's day only to be met with one-word answers while Nicola tapped away at her tablet or iPhone. And she could tell from the pictures, framed and mounted on the off-yellow walls of the house, that not only was Nicola prized by both her father and her mother, but she and her mother had once been quite close. There were fewer pictures of them together the older Nicola got.

Would she have been like Nicola if her own mother had lived or would she still be clinging to her, grateful to have her in her life? No way to know really. And as for a father, like Shaka, she'd never really had one to miss him.

"Hey, no brooding. Vibes up yourself," Nicola said, snapping her out of her reverie.

Zahara laughed when she saw that her friend had finished off her already dramatic risqué look with a startling red wig.

Nicola tossed her head, unoffended, chanting the lyrics to that silly and infectious song, "Whip My Hair" as they geared up to leave.

When they descended the stairs to where Nicola's mother was already waiting with her keys, Zahara half-expected her to tell Nicola to take off the wig, and to ask them, as Granny Linda would have, "Where's the rest of your clothes?" But she didn't.

"You ready, girls?" was all she said. "Nicola, don't forget your phone, I don't want to have to be looking for you all night once the show's over."

Zahara used her own phone to text Shaka.

On our way.

He texted back that he'd wait for her by the east entrance to the grounds.

His mouth dropped when he saw her but she couldn't tell if he was pleased or just surprised.

Kong whistled and then Monkey and the others did as well. She blushed. She reached for Shaka's hand as they headed inside. He still hadn't said anything.

Just inside the gate, they met up with Dan. He'd swapped his plaid pants for jeans; all the boys were wearing jeans, jeans and t-shirts, making her feel like a bit of a peacock walking amongst them. Once the music started though, she got over her discomfort.

The night started with a DJ contest which the Lion Crew loved, boasting how someday they'd be the baddest sound in the land. The contest gave the crowd a chance to get hyped up and go crazy singing and dancing to their favourite soca tunes. Shaka and Monkey and the rest of them sparred, Step Up style, and Nicola showed off a little too while Zahara and Dan laughed and rolled their eyes at their antics.

Zahara took off the dainty slingbacks Nicola had forced her to wear, when her brown, blue and yellow Dereon sneakers wouldn't fit Zahara's feet. Her heel hung off the sling backs and the heel, short though it was, was too high for Zahara and forced her to move too carefully to truly relax. After taking them off she danced in the cool grass.

Shaka took her arm and attempted to twirl her around in a ballroom move but she knew she wasn't as graceful as Nicola. Although Nicola wasn't exactly the picture of grace just then as she pushed back on Dan, wining while he stood stoically, letting her do her thing.

When Claudette 'CP' Peters, Zahara's soca idol came on, Zahara almost lost her mind. She rushed closer to the stage where there was no grass and her toes were in real danger of getting trampled by thousands of jumping feet but she still couldn't see until Shaka lifted her up onto his shoulders as though she weighed nothing at all. She didn't even have time to be self-conscious. She was acting completely out of character but ... *Claudette Peters!* The woman was as stunning in person as she'd imagined, as she moved her waist and swung her locs.

Zahara was cheering as wildly as everyone around her and waving an inflated tube although she wasn't sure how she'd ended up with one. She was screaming her throat raw, and somewhere inside she'd already decided that this was the best night ever, like she couldn't possibly be as happy ever again as she was in that moment.

Later, as they made their way out the grounds, Shaka had to carry her on his back because someone had wandered off with the slingbacks, or she'd forgotten where she'd left them. She was amazed that Nicola didn't seem to mind; Granny Linda would never stand for her losing her things like that. Nicola leaned up against some random car with Dan, her back against the door, his hands on the roof over her head, as they kissed. Shaka put her down where it was grassy and as they waited for Nicola's mother, she shifted, suddenly uncomfortable.

"You don't like my outfit," she said.

"Is not that," he said. She felt his arm brush against hers as he shifted from one foot to the other, as though nervous. "You look hot, don't get me wrong…it's just…it's not you that's all."

And she felt embarrassed, because he was right. It *wasn't* her. She was like a kid playing dress up.

"And what going on with the tiger eyes?" he teased.

She laughed, because, yeah, she had to agree with him there. Nicola *had* gone a little crazy with the eye makeup.

"Ask Nicola," she said.

"But is you let her do it."

She only shrugged at that. It was true; it wasn't like she'd said 'No' when Nicola had come at her with her triple decker make up kit with its many colours and pull out drawers. Maybe a part of her had wanted to try it all on—the "hot gyal" look—to see what all the fuss was about.

Just then Nicola's mother pulled up and Dan and Nicola broke apart though not in any particular hurry. Zahara couldn't even imagine holding a boy's hand in front of Granny Linda much less kissing one. Nicola's life was like a whole different world.

Shaka leaned down for a quick kiss though, just a peck, as if he knew she felt self-conscious or maybe felt so himself. He squeezed her hand before walking back over to his boys, and she tiptoed on bare feet to the waiting vehicle.

Chapter 18

"I have a rap for your project," he said the next time he saw her, after Carnival.

It was called 'My Name is Melanin' and it was written like a letter from Melanin to folks who bleached and didn't realize how bad they looked because of it, or how much damage they were doing to themselves, asking them to re-think the consequences.

"Don't be like Michael, Kartel, or Sosa…"

"I wrote it over that melody you play me the other day," he told her. "The one I record on my phone. Remember you say how you want a soundtrack for the project? Well this could be it." He paused. "I was also thinking we could make it into a music video."

"A music video?" she asked incredulously.

"Yeah," he said, trying to sound as if a music video was the obvious thing to do. "Play to your strengths. We can record it together."

She was already shaking her head when they heard Call Me Ted's voice right behind them.

"You should do it."

They were on the gallery, in their informal groups, waiting for Mr. Perry to come and open the building. Presumably, Ted must have been listening in on their conversation. Shaka watched Zahara's expression change from irritation to amusement when Kong asked, "Hey, wha' fu you story, anyway?" He sounded more curious than challenging.

"My story?" Call Me Ted said.

"Yeah, where you from?"

Ted hesitated and looked offended.

"Antigua," he said, finally.

Kong held up his palms. "No disrespect, but arwe nar exactly swim inna ching chung."

Ted's lips twitched at Kong's indiscreet and offensive response, as everyone else within hearing distance, Shaka and Zahara included, cringed.

Kong was oblivious.

"What?" he sang out, offended, when Accident elbowed him.

155

"You can't say that," Scaly said.

Kong rolled his eyes. "Call Me Ted know me nuh mean nothing, jack. Stop acting like a girl."

"Hey!" more than one girl said at once.

"Jesus," Kong said. "Aryuh thin-skin bad."

By this time Ted was giggling. He waved off all the outrage.

"It's cool, it's cool," he said. Then added, "I'm of Chinese descent but ah ya me barn."

Kong bent over laughing at that, and when he straightened up, bumped fists with Ted.

"Alright, boss," he said, still chuckling.

"My parents, they own the convenience store at the bottom of the city, near the harbour, across from the parking lot. They were among the first to come here in the eighties when the Caribbean and China open up relations. They come from the Mingshan region. I been there only once. Couldn't wait to come home."

"Seen," Kong said, and turned back to Scaly and the others.

'Yeah," Ted said. With Kong's attention now re-directed elsewhere, Shaka took the opportunity to press the older boy on the song's possibilities.

"You think we should record it for real, for real?"

He knew that Ted was already involved in music production.

"We could," Ted said. "Me like novelty songs like that, you know, songs outside the norm."

"Let's do it," Zahara blurted out.

He stared at her, disbelieving. She looked as surprised as he felt but even as he watched, he saw her start to nod, quickly taking to the idea. She smiled—God, he loved her smile—with certainty when she said, "Yeah, let's!"

He turned to Ted, smiling now too.

"So wha' we have to do?" he asked.

Plans to record the song moved into action surprisingly quickly. Ted booked studio time at the independent label he worked with. The environment at the studio was informal. That was definitely a plus because it meant a couple of kids could be brought in on a whim a few evenings. On the downside it meant they were never quite sure when they'd have the equipment to themselves. It worked out somehow though.

In the studio, he and his boys lounged on bean bag chairs refining their rap, while Ted divided his time between the keyboard and the soundboard. It was easy

Joanne C. Hillhouse

to lose track of time in the dim room, especially when Ted continuously had Zahara and Nicola on repeat in the sound booth– "Again!"– playing and singing, even harmonizing a little. The girls had collaborated on a hook, Zahara's muted, somewhat raspy tone providing the perfect counterpoint to Nicola's soaring vocals.

He'd often pause what he was doing just to watch her and record a bit of her singing alongside Nicola on his phone. He told himself it was for the project. The boys teased him, of course. Kong, especially, would lean in and whisper in his ear, in falsetto, "mi gyal pretty bad, see, she like a shooting star."

He'd push his friend and his hot breath away, eyes still on his girl; checking the way her dimple winked in and out as she sang, the way her eyes looked alive. She was beautiful, and he was lucky she'd even given him the time of day. The way she and Nicola worked with each other, rearranging vocals for a tighter harmonic fit, or just giggled, arms thrown around each other's shoulders, like they'd been friends for ever instead of just three fourths of a summer, was also evidence of her stepping out of her shell. That was nice to see too.

It was good, too, that her Granny Linda wasn't giving her grief about the extra time away from home. She'd joked that Nicola's mother must've worked some

158

kind of obeah on Granny Linda because, since Party Monarch, as long as Nicola's mother asked, the answer was 'yes.' That's two things he had to thank Nicola for, even though the girl still treated him like he was something sticky under her shoe. Three things: because she was talented, and she had gotten over herself enough for them to make a connection as Granny and Anansi. They were going to be great …if he did say so himself.

The first time he heard his song on the radio, he was doing the dishes after dinner while his mother moved around their small kitchen, putting things away. Pappy was in his chair in the living room, radio turned up on the news, about the only reason he put on the radio since he couldn't stand modern music or chatty DJs. Zahara complained that her Granny Linda always changed the station when music came on; must be an old people thing because as soon as the news presenter signed off, Pappy started making getting up noises. That's when "Melanin" cut in and though he'd given the CD to Diva himself, Shaka's body seized up in shock. It was noticeable enough for his mother to ask, "Something wrong? Wha' happen?" And he screamed, he wasn't even ashamed to say it, he screamed, and ran into the living room, pushing past Pappy to turn up the radio as loud as it could go.

"You bwoy!" Pappy chastised.

"That's my song, that's my song," he shouted, and that shut up both Pappy and his mother who had come out from the kitchen with more questions.

He couldn't stand still; dashed to his room, got his phone and started texting everybody. Zahara first, then the Crew.

Put on the radio. Melanninnn!!!!

His phone started ringing right away, Zahara's voice excited and breathy on the other end.

"It sound like a real song," she said.

"It is a real song!"

"I know, I know but..." He didn't have any more words, and apparently neither did she, and he pictured her standing there, in the bedroom he'd never seen, just like he was in his, phone pressed to his ear, listening to this thing they'd been a part of creating, together. The song finished and Diva started bigging him up when he heard Granny Linda's voice on Zahara's end, "Wait, who move my radio!?"

"Gotta go," his girlfriend said and she was gone.

"When it's nice we play it twice," Diva continued on the radio. "Shout out to mi sparring, even though he throw me 'way all summer…here it is again, 'Mela-nin'." And he was grinning at her words as the music started up again.

Though the radio was loud enough for him to hear it throughout the house, he was drawn back to the living room, where his mother and Pappy were standing much as he'd left them.

"You made this?" his mother asked. And she sounded so surprised he was almost insulted.

What did she think he was up to with the lap top and the digital recorder and all the music he bought or borrowed? What did she think he'd been doing at the Culture Department all summer? Choops, on the inside, since he wouldn't forget the care of his brain to suck his teeth at his mother for real. Besides, he was too happy to be upset.

"Yes," he said. "We made that. Me, the Crew, Zahara, Nicola, Call me Ted…" He was rambling now, and still, grinning, but he couldn't help himself.

His mother was smiling, his grandfather too. In fact, Pappy started to bop a little bit to the music, and wasn't that a sight. He had the presence of mind to record a few seconds of Pappy bopping, the song still running in the background, using his phone. The boys nearly killed themselves laughing when he showed it to them the next day on the walk to rehearsals.

161

"Pappy ha moves man," Kong joked.

When they got to rehearsal and he finally got Za-hara alone after all the back patting and "congratulations" from the other members of the cast, he showed her the video of Pappy as well.

She laughed and said, "Well, Granny Linda definitely didn't dance, but once I explained why I touched her precious radio, she didn't turn the station when the song came on again."

He joked, "For her that's a ringing endorsement, ent?"

"Ah dah me say!" Zahara agreed, as they both laughed out loud, still giddy with the excitement of having a song on the radio.

Chapter 19

The week the Melanin song dropped, they moved their rehearsals into the theatre where they would be putting on their adaptation of *The Dancing Granny*.

The design team had clearly been busy. Patterns had been drawn onto the stage floor, lines and circles and rows to represent the earth. The backdrop featured trees cut out of paperboard and a backdrop of canvas painted beautifully with blue swirls for the sky. The set looked spectacular. Zahara couldn't believe they'd been working on it the whole time.

The wardrobe mistress had come as well with their costumes which she'd labelled and hung up backstage on portable clothes racks. Granny's costume was a loose, flowing Africa-inspired dress, with a distinctive yellow and green pattern and matching headwrap. The dress draped in such a way that, once they'd finished tugging and tucking, it made Nicola looked more vixen-like than any grandmother Zahara had ever seen.

Anansi's mother-in-law would be wearing a house-coat made of fabric from the same colour palette. The most outstanding ladies' costume, though, was worn by Anansi's wife; a black evening gown made of yards of netting giving the illusion of a spider's web. For most of the play Anansi's wife would sit perched in her chair, a special prop designed to look like a spider-web and built by Wanga, the celebrated Carnival costume de-signer. It reminded Zahara a little of Pappy's chair in that, she suspected no one but Mrs. Anansi would be allowed to sit in the 'web'.

Anansi's crew of backing dancers were outfitted in black unitards decorated with florescent yellow and green paint that would glow under the black lights. But the face masks were the genius part of their costumes. Where the noses would have been, the masks had branches sticking out—tree limbs covered with leaves so that the Lion Crew could be onstage all the time, blending in and out of the scenery as needed. It was kind of creepy actually; and Zahara found she couldn't stare directly at them for too long. Of course, once they realized this, they had to tease her by creeping up on her with the masks. She found herself running around backstage like a mad woman until Mr. Perry yelled at them to focus.

"We only have one week left, people!"

Shaka meanwhile, was having fun with his dread-locced wig which he swung this way and that.

"Who me look like, Bob Marley or Maxi Priest?" Then he started bouncing and shaking his locs like the Rastafarians did when the spirit moved them and the herb hit them. The locs looked like spider legs coming out of his head. It matched perfectly with the rest of his costume, a black unitard with webs and spiders sewn all over it. Someone said it looked like a superhero's costume.

A heated debate about what superpowers Anansi would have if he had superpowers followed. That got them talking about Peter Parker and Spiderman and pretty soon they were almost arguing over the all-important question of who would beat who in a battle to the death – Superman or Wolverine, the Incredible Hulk or Juggernaut, Batman or Iron Man? Shaka insisted that Batman and Iron Man weren't even real superheroes, just rich men with too much money, plenty toys, big egos, and "bags ah crazy." The discussion got louder and more intense than it should have considering the subject matter.

Zahara looked around for Mr. Perry wondering how come he hadn't yelled at them to keep down the noise. Mr. Perry, it seemed, was having an argument of his own, with the wardrobe mistress.

He wasn't pleased with the Anansi costume.

"It's too much spider, not enough man," he said sharply. "The whole point is that we're breaking with the idea of them being animal characters. They're not animals, just animal-*like*. This works for the spider dance number but not for anything else."

The wardrobe mistress was a short white woman with greying hair who'd been introduced as Ms. Berkeley. She'd worked in theatre in New York before retiring to Antigua with her stockbroker husband. Not only had she convinced her friends from the expat community to donate money to the production, she was working with the production as a form of voluntary community service. Zahara looked on as Mr. Perry ranted and wondered why Ms. Berkeley didn't just walk away. It was weird seeing Mr. Perry in hysterics; he usually had it together. Ms. Berkeley stayed calm, only patting him on the arm as if to say without really saying, "Don't worry, sec, it'll all work out." Zahara wondered if the wardrobe mistress was used to high-strung theatre types.

She sat in a corner next to the stage watching it all and feeling unaccountably happy. Dan walked over looking ridiculous in the white spidery mesh top and shiny black pants that was to be the band's uniform. He didn't look happy about it either. She tried not to laugh.

She was wearing the female version of the look. Underneath the artfully-ripped oversized mesh, she had on black rocker shorts and a bustier, clothing she'd have been too self-conscious to wear once upon a time. She especially liked her black boots which came about two-thirds of the way up her shin. She felt very "rock 'n roll." Prince would approve.

"You at least look good in yours," Dan confirmed.

"You think I look good?" she teased.

"Oh, now you wan flirt with me? Now me off the market," he joked, forgetting his issues with the ward-robe for the minute.

She smiled. He was so much easier to be around post-Nicola. She should've known her friend wouldn't put up with any of his obnoxiousness.

Chapter 20

"These are your children. Do you think you can just hand them over to me and don't look back?" Mr. Perry paced as he spoke.

Shaka was familiar with this version of his English teacher; it was the version he and others in his class saw when they didn't complete an assignment or work up to expectations. It was Mr. Perry's "if you don't do better, you're letting yourselves down" voice. It was funny to see parents on the receiving end of it.

He was sitting with Zahara and the others on the stage. The cast and crew's parents were spread out among the rows of seats in the theatre, but many of the seats were empty.

"Look here," Mr. Perry continued. "Near thirty of them between front and backstage, and how many of you?"

Only about half of the parents had shown up by Shaka's count. To be fair though, some, like his mother, couldn't attend because they had to work. Those who didn't work or who'd been able to get off work early were still trickling in. Every few minutes or so, the door at the back of the room creaked as another parent entered.

Apparently Mr. Perry wasn't interested in being fair.

"I don't accept tardiness from my students. Their schools don't accept tardiness and truancy from them. You expect them to be where you tell them, when you tell them don't you? So, are we wrong to expect the same of you?"

Shaka watched, almost in awe, as Mr. Perry paused and looked down his nose at the parents like they disgusted him. The weird thing was they took it. The parents shifted uncomfortably in their seats but didn't make a peep.

Mr. Perry's superpower, he'd discovered, was the ability to command an entire room of people even if it was a roomful of parents, parents who probably earned lots more than he did. He wasn't exactly sure what a teacher's salary was but he knew the Teachers Union was always in the news complaining about too-low wages, so it couldn't be very much. He knew that all the kids in their theatre troupe didn't come from the same world. Some of their worlds were within reach of each other sure, like his and Zahara's, but others like Dan's and Nicola's might as well be as far away as the moon with their helpers and nannies and whatnot.

But Mr. Perry wasn't checking for any of that just now. He was letting the parents have it as though their deep pockets didn't matter.

Shaka looked around and noted that he wasn't the only one up on the stage doing a shift-and-shuffle to keep from laughing.

"Have I asked you for a single cent all summer?" Mr. Perry demanded, switching gears. "Have you volunteered more than the mere minimum, some of you, of dropping your kids off and picking them up? Offered another kid a ride maybe? Have any of you said, 'Hey, Mr. Perry can I help out with snacks?'"

Mr. Perry paused to let them all ponder.

"Did it ever occur to any of you that I might be doing this for free? You ever stopped to ask if the Culture Department is paying Mr. Perry for his time?"

Mr. Perry made a scoffing sound. Though Shaka could only see the back of the teacher's head, the way that head swivelled slowly as Mr. Perry stood arms akimbo made it clear he was meeting the parent's gaze as though daring them to answer him. None did.

"Since you asked, the answers are *no, no, no,* and no." He ticked the "no's" off on his fingers as he spoke, holding up his open palm when he was done. And then with a shift of his stance, a wave of the palm, his whole attitude changed.

"But we're not here for that...who did or didn't do what. What you need to know is that your children have done amazing work this summer, and this Saturday it all comes to a climax right here in this space."

A hush fell on the room then as Mr. Perry paused to let his words sink in. Shaka felt a chill run though his body. For perhaps the first time in his life, he, a natural performer, felt nerves uncurl like a giant snake having itself a good stretch in his stomach.

He looked across at Zahara. Sitting there with Dan the Man and Call Me Ted, she looked so much more at ease than when they'd first met. Even a week ago she hadn't been this confident. He was happy that he'd had a hand in helping her see what she was capable of. He just hoped he had some *rah!rah!rah!* left over for himself, because suddenly he felt like he might vomit. He swallowed. That would be embarrassing.

"What we're here for right now," Mr. Perry continued, "is to find out what you can do. No, what you *will* do going forward. And I don't mean buy a ticket to come out to the show because that's a given."

It actually wasn't though. How many school shows had he and the Crew performed in where parents were noticeably absent? As though someone had hung a sign on the door saying, 'kids only'. He understood, and suspected the parents did as well, that Mr. Perry was saying "you better be there."

"Now let's hear what else you're prepared to do."

No hands shot up, no one volunteered; but Mr. Perry seemed to expect that.

"Sherri," he said, calling the girl who, as production secretary, had been his silent shadow all summer, keeping track of everything. She was a mouse of a girl from one of the deep country schools. Shaka had never given her much thought except to wonder briefly why someone would join a theatrical production to take notes. She was a familiar sight stepping forward with her clipboard and pen.

"Beginning at this end," Mr Perry said pointing to a parent in the front row, "and continuing until we

172

reach the back, each parent is going to tell me what you are prepared to give."

There were no "if's" and "but's" about it; it was clear Mr. Perry meant business and wouldn't take no for an answer. Sherri started writing as the chastened parents started making their pledges. Still in the midst of his mini freak out, Shaka wasn't paying attention to the process, but his neck snapped up at the sound of Pappy's voice.

"I could help out with transportation."

He didn't know how he'd missed his grandfather's entry. Pappy might be lanky but he was tall and had presence. Not to mention that old-fashioned straw hat he always wore.

"I can carry kids in my car," Pappy was saying. "But if you all need more I can get some of the other guys from the taxi stand to help out."

"Oh, that'll come in handy," Mr. Perry replied. "Rehearsals will be running late as we come down to the wire this week. It'll be good to have a taxi service on speed dial. Give Sherri the numbers before you leave."

Pappy nodded and sat back down, his hat in his lap. His eyes found Shaka's. Pappy propped his chin in his hand with a little smirk followed by a lip tug that

Shaka interpreted as "pull up your lip." It was something his grandfather often did and said when his grandson's mouth fell open, as it was now, in surprise.

He hadn't read the note Mr. Perry had made them take home but now he wished he had. *What had the drama teacher threatened to get even Pappy to show up?*

He heard a gasp from Zahara. When he looked across he saw a similar gobsmacked look on her face. He followed her eyes to where a woman about Pappy's age had stood up. The woman wore a navy pantsuit and looked like she'd just come from work.

"I can help with snacks," the woman was saying. "Finger foods for during rehearsals and performance night."

The woman seemed almost shy. *Was that Granny Linda?* He'd pictured someone taller. Her voice had sort of a shake in it too. This was Zahara's no nonsense, 'take no bullshit' grandmother? *Wow.*

"Maybe some grilled pork and pineapple skewers?" she added.

"That sounds good," Mr. Perry said nodding. "Although you know, some of the kids are vegetarian; pork might not do for everyone."

"That's okay, I can substitute chicken," Granny Linda said, and at that everyone fell out laughing.

When the parents were dismissed and the cast was told to "take five", Shaka started moving in Pappy's direction. As he approached, he saw that Pappy had company. Zahara's grandmother. Zahara, who presumably had been heading toward her grandmother, came to a dead stop next to him. They looked at each other, faces mirroring surprise.

Who knew they even knew each other? But apparently they not only knew each other, they were hugging-friends, because that's what they were doing when he turned back toward them. Pappy was bent over and Granny Linda was leaning up and into him. It was deep but fairly quick, thank God, because he shuddered at where his mind automatically went at the sight of his grandfather and his girlfriend's grandmother being affectionate with each other.

He was close enough to hear Pappy say, "Long time, Lin, how do?" in a voice sweet-sweet like sugar cake. That, too, was startling, as even Pappy's jokes were rough.

"Long time, Errol," Granny Linda, or, apparently, Lin, responded.

They didn't say much else, just stared at each other like people mapping the changes; each line, each grey hair, searching for something youthful and familiar.

175

The thought that that could be him and Zahara some-day made him shudder.

Long after the parents had left, as they were pre-paring for a long night of run-throughs and tweaking, one of many that week, Shaka whispered, still shocked, about as shocked as Zahara looked, "Pappy say he used to check for her in school…he also say Antigua too damn small."

"You know what this mean, right?" Kong said as they walked to practice the next day. "You and Z coulda been cousins." Then, as though saying it made it so, he made a whooping sound. "Kinky! Ole bwoy have ah t'ing for his cousin."

"That's sick," Accident said.

"Not really, it don't matter as long as they not first cousins," said Big Head. They looked at him funny.

"First of all, she's not my cousin," he began.

"That you *know of*," Kong interrupted.

"She's not my cousin. Second of all," he contin-ued, "that thing between Pappy and her Granny was a long time ago."

"Yeah, otherwise we'd be talking 'bout old people sex and that's just gross," Scaly said.

Monkey did a full body shudder. "Come on, dude, now you have me thinking 'bout old people sex."

"Speaking of which, she give you any yet?" asked Big Head.

"Please! The two of them should write a song called 'Virgin 'til I Die'," Kong said grinning.

"Because you have *soooo* much experience?" he countered.

"More than *you*."

"Whatever," he said, abandoning the argument. So what if it was true? For all their big talk, none of them had done much. Last year, Kong had made out with that girl Kammy during a school field trip at Long Bay. He hadn't been able to stop boasting about it, though it hadn't gone very far and Kammy had since pretended Kong didn't even exist.

Anyway, he had other things on his mind besides Kong's never-ending game of one-upmanship. And for the first time, he didn't feel like sharing his thoughts with his boys. He was still thinking about Pappy and Granny Linda.

That morning, he'd confronted his grandfather before he could take off for work. He'd boiled a strip of cocoa and sweetened it the way he knew Pappy liked, letting the scent lure him out of his room. When they were seated and slurping at the dining table, he'd asked for the story of Pappy and 'Lin'.

"She was a pretty little thing," Pappy said after a moment, and, no, that wasn't weird at all, listening to his grandfather moon over his girlfriend's grandmother, lips quirked in fond memory. Thankfully Pappy hadn't lingered there.

Apparently, Pappy hadn't seen Granny Linda since her daughter's funeral.

"Knew who that girl was soon as you started bringing her round," Pappy had said. According to his grandfather, the fact that he'd even gone to Sheena's funeral was one of the bigger secrets between Pappy and Shaka's mother. Shaka had tensed at that.

Why would his mother care whose funeral Pappy went to… unless… Had Pappy cheated on his grandmother with Granny Linda-also-known-as-Lin? He barely remembered his grandmother; she'd died when he was little. He felt like he'd stepped into a soap opera.

But, no, that wasn't it.

"Lin's daughter was wild," Pappy had said. "Wild and spoiled. Took what she want, did what she want, left destruction behind her, and didn't look back to see it. She attracted lots of interest from both man and woman, the man an' them wanting to…well, you know…and the woman and them hating her because she didn't have to try you know, she was so pretty. And she didn't care who a man belonged to."

Pappy had paused for a long time then, as though trying to decide if to go further. Shaka had held his breath feeling like he'd explode if Pappy didn't go on.

"Lin used to be the same way," Pappy had finally continued. "Not as selfish perhaps, but like a butterfly, you know, no boy could hold on to her for long. I tried but she slipped from my grasp the same way she did with others who tried to tie her down. In fact, it wasn't til she get wi' chile that she settle. Didn't marry nobody or nothing, not even the father, who was probably happy not to have to stick around. If she even knew who he was.

"She was fast, ah not goin' lie. But finally there was something she couldn't run 'way from. I'd see her from time to time and it was like she had erased all that she'd been before. But maybe the wildness was in the blood because she never had a firm hand on that child of hers, not the way she do on her granddaughter."

Granny Linda's strictness began to make a kind of sense to Shaka as he listened to Pappy talk. He had assumed Zahara's grandmother was just a "spare the rod, spoil the child" brand of parent. His mother was like that sometimes, but maybe she had her reasons as well.

The whole story was a lot to process, and Pappy wasn't nearly done.

"Your father was seeing Zahara's mother on the side. Is she he was with, coming from some Carnival show, when the accident happened." Pappy had paused again then. He'd never seen his grandfather look so sad, but when he spoke again there was a trace of anger in his voice. "Your father was drunk off his ass as usual and had no business behind the wheel of a car, when the two o' dem run into a tree. Only good thing to come from that mess was they didn't kill nobody else."

He had so many questions even after talking with Pappy. But his grandfather, though he'd clearly been prepared for his grandson's questions and had always been someone Shaka could talk to, had his limits. His father would always be a sore spot. If Shaka was un-moved by the memory, his grandfather was often moved to anger. Now he had a greater understanding why.

"Last time I saw Lin was at her daughter funeral. We didn't talk. Don't know why I went. Know Wendy would've been hurt if she knew I went, with me being her father and Lin daughter being the keep-woman for your no-good father, God rest his soul. Everything was so fresh…and she was in so much pain, your mother, feeling shame that rightfully wasn't hers. This woulda just been…more.

"Everybody was just broken down 'round that time…Lin looked like a shell at the funeral, didn't bring her granddaughter with her, didn't have no husband, just looked alone. I come back home and your mother moving 'round like a ghost. You don't know your ass from your elbow all then. I had to be her father like I hadn't had to be since she was a little girl and I had to be a father to you a kinda how…I think I did okay there, you come good…and eventually she come…well not back to herself, she still carry plenty pain, but she also carry on, like we all have to do. Like I had to do after cancer take your grandmother from me."

After that, he shut down altogether and put on the Blues. Talk of his late wife always did that to him. He didn't go in to work that day.

Shaka didn't know what he should tell Zahara.

On the one hand, she deserved to know everything but thinking over Pappy's pain, and his mother's, even her Granny Linda's, he couldn't help thinking it wasn't his story to tell. These things weighing on him, he wasn't exactly himself as he dragged his feet to re-hearsals that afternoon after the heart-to-heart with Pappy.

Chapter 21

Zahara and Shaka sat shoulder to shoulder on the wall surrounding the theatre, a bit apart from the others as they waited for the caretaker to arrive with the keys. Mr. Perry was pacing, his phone at his ear.

"He better mind he heart nuh explode before the week out," Shaka joked weakly.

She reached under the foil covering the tray sitting next to her, grabbed one of the veggie pineapple skewers, and passed it to him.

As promised, Granny Linda had made snacks for them, but if Zahara thought her grandmother would share her secrets as readily as her food, she was wrong. That morning, Granny Linda had left for work before Zahara was even up. She'd found the snacks and a note on the kitchen counter.

Shaka bit off a few chunks of roasted vegetables, "It's like eating a health popsicle."

"Thank God she got the memo that vegetarian don't mean, 'don't eat pork.'"

They both chuckled at that.

"So weird seeing her with your grandfather yesterday. Her little vanishing act this morning make me feel there's something she not telling me."

She and Granny Linda didn't talk about stuff, not like Shaka and his grandfather. It was no surprise, she supposed, that there were things she didn't know about her grandmother. It had been enough, most of her life, just to know Granny Linda was there, solid and unmovable. And while it sometimes made her feel like she was in prison, she also felt protected. Growing up without parents, Granny Linda had been her one sure thing. She was grateful, but lately she found she wanted more, more than just rules and consequences. It made her a little sad to think maybe it was too late for that.

Beside her, Shaka took a deep breath and swallowed the last of his pineapple. He looked like he had something important to tell her. But nothing could have prepared her for what came next.

"My father and your mother were together the night they died."

"What?"

"I always knew he wasn't alone when he died. That he was with a woman he was seeing on the side. Nobody talk about him, or about that night, but you hear things, you know. But Pappy tell me who the other smadee was when I ask 'bout him and your Granny Linda today. Was your mother."

She turned it over and over in her mind and it still didn't make any sense.

"Okay, what?" she asked again, blinking.

And he told her everything Pappy had told him. His father, her mother, Granny Linda as someone young and fun and embracing life—she couldn't wrap her mind around any of it, and yet somehow it made a kind of sense. They were interrupted by the arrival of the caretaker and by Mr. Perry calling for them to come together.

Practice was a disaster. Their run-through of the musical from start to finish, something that should have taken an hour, took five. Mr. Perry kept interrupting the actors to shout critiques.

"Are you guys kidding me?" he finally snapped. "At this stage in the game, this is what you're putting on, this lacklustre bull..." And on like that. It was a disaster.

But thankfully, as distracted as her thoughts were, her fingers mostly remembered what they were supposed to do even if her heart wasn't in it and her mind was otherwise occupied.

She couldn't stop turning Pappy's confessions around and around in her mind. She felt as if the world as she knew it had come to an end. She was having difficulty hitting the re-set button on reality.

Even more disturbing were the "what ifs" she couldn't shake.

Like *what if* she had the wildness in her too? After all, hadn't she snuck out and lied and already done so many things she wouldn't normally do this summer? Wasn't her heart even now filled with defiance and, much as she tried to ignore it, a growing sort of craving for something more with Shaka?

And the thought of Shaka brought her to the biggest "what" if of all. If what Pappy had said was true, then her mother and Shaka's father had been a "thing." So, what if Shaka's father was also her father? After all she'd never met her father; Granny Linda had never spoken of him. She supposed it could be Shaka's father as well as anybody else.

"Nah," Shaka said, after practice as they waited for the volunteer taxi men who were picking up those without transportation. "You were already a little girl when they were seeing each other."

"Yeah, but we don't know how long they were seeing each other," she said.

"If it was so, Pappy woulda said something from the first time you start coming around. The fact that he didn't mean nothing there to tell."

"That, or he didn't know."

Shaka groaned. "You goin' drive yourself crazy with this. The boys an' dem already grinding me 'bout us being cousins because of your grandmother and Pappy now you want to raise the stakes to what if we are brother an' sister? Seriously?"

Put like that, it did sound kind of farfetched.

Just then Pappy drove up with two other taxis trailing him, effectively ending their conversation.

It was late by the time she got home. Granny Linda was still up, as expected; her grandmother wouldn't sleep, never did, until she was in the house.

"I leave some bush tea on the counter for you," was her only greeting before she turned toward her room. As Zahara watched her go, something pulled at her.

She sat on the couch in the living room, the TV on mute flashing at her but not holding her attention, as she plucked her guitar and sipped the slightly too-sweet tea. This was how her mother used to make it, letting her scoop up the sugar at the bottom with her fingers, while Granny Linda fussed that she was going to rot her teeth.

"That's okay, it's just baby teeth," she remembered her mother joking. Maybe it was a memory; maybe just a story her mind made up to fill the empty spaces.

She wondered if that's how her mother had been: funny. If that's how she defused whatever tension there must surely have been between her and Granny Linda, with humour. It was something else she might never know. For all she'd learned that day, it felt like all she had was more questions.

She remembered how her first crush Lauréna Lee used to sweep away their imaginations with her tall tales. She wanted to believe everything that had happened this past week was just another tall tale. But that way of thinking was a slippery slope, wasn't it? Because if this week of uncomfortable revelations was a nightmare then maybe the whole summer was a dream, and she didn't want that. This summer, she'd not only made friends, learned a lot, and shared something special with a boy she really, really liked. She'd begun to come out of her shell as a musician, embracing that whatever streak of wildness she might have inherited from her mother and, as it turned out, Granny Linda, didn't have to be a bad thing. It made her feel like she could do what Prince did: get up on stage and make people feel things. It scared her too a little bit, but she didn't want to give it up either. She didn't want to go back to being a part of the scenery. She had things to express, and she liked feeling free to express them.

And as she mulled over these things, her fingers continued to dance, pulling sound from the strings, sounds that somehow became music. Slowly, she began to tune into the melody pouring out of her. It brought a smile to her lips, quickened her heart. Yes, she made this. She didn't know what other songs were inside of her, but she wanted to find out.

The tea was cold by the time she got up from the couch. She took the cup to the sink, poured out the remains, feeling a prick of guilt at the wastefulness. It was a tiny bit of rebellion that she kept pouring anyway.

She knocked at Granny Linda's door, her other hand squeezing the neck of the guitar much too tightly. She pushed the door open, causing the medals to clatter against each other. As much as she battened down the rest of the house, Granny Linda never locked her own door; but even as a child Zahara had known not to enter without good reason or permission.

She stepped in just as her grandmother turned over in her bed. Granny Linda squinted at her in the dark. Zahara's hand moved toward the light switch, but she didn't turn it on. She found she couldn't say what had built up in her to say with the lights on and Granny Linda glaring at her.

"Who's my father?"

And it got as quiet and still as it could get. The only sound was the rustling of bed sheets and the squeaking of bed springs as Granny Linda sat up until her legs were hanging over the side of the bed. She just sat there though, not saying anything.

Zahara knew she was crossing one of the many lines Granny Linda had drawn, and wasn't that what she'd been getting into trouble for all summer? She wanted to turn and run away but instead she went and sat beside Granny Linda on the bed. She wasn't sure what she'd expected when Granny Linda drew a breath, finally, but a straight up answer wasn't it.

"His name was Sylvester."

"Sylvester?"

"Yes."

"Is that the man she was with when she...?" Zahara started to ask but Granny Linda cut her off.

"No. That..." It was clear she didn't even want to say his name. "No," she said again. "She had only been running with that one a couple of months. You wouldn't have seen him because she knew better than to bring a married man 'round me. But no, you were already there, underfoot, by the time she started running with that one. I raised her better than the company she was keeping but by then like she didn't care 'bout nothing."

Granny Linda sounded sad, and, Zahara realized for the first time, guilty, like her daughter's sins were hers to carry. Even Zahara knew that was bull. Everyone was responsible for their own choices. Whatever her mother had been running from, Granny Linda couldn't have stopped her. But was Zahara's father the thing she'd been running from?

"She and my father...Sylvester...had a falling out or something? He was bad to her?"

"No, no, no," Granny Linda corrected. "Sylvester was a good boy...a good boy. But some women don't know a good thing when it right in front of them. Your mother was like that." Granny Linda sighed. "And maybe she got that from me."

"Where is he?"

"I don't know."

Was that fondness she heard in Granny Linda's voice?

"I kept expecting you to ask about him as you got older, but you never did, and I wasn't sure what I'd say anyway. And then when you picked up that guitar…"

"He was a guitar player?

"A hell of a guitar player, yes!" Granny Linda actually chuckled. "And yes, it used to be his."

Now she was pretty sure Granny Linda had liked her father. She could hear it in her voice. She suddenly understood why Granny Linda had been so resistant to her picking up the guitar. She'd thought it was about her mother, about memories of her mother being too painful…but if it the Stella Harmony had been her father's, maybe it was something else. But what?

"What happened?"

Granny Linda sighed. "Everything your mother did was my doing," she said. "I was too young when I had her, too spoiled and wilful myself. It can be attractive to a man at first but in the end what many men want is a woman they can tame and Sheena was untamable. She loved Sylvester but still…" Granny Linda sighed heavily again.

When she continued she spoke slowly, her voice shaky in the darkness.

"He was like a son to me, that one. He didn't have nobody else here, not really. He came over from Dominica with only the shirt on his back and that guitar. He gave it to her after he started catching his hand and got an electric one, 'cause the bands that paid weren't into that acoustic stuff. Daytime he worked in construction and he played with the band an' them at night, weekends too. I guess she liked who he was when he was up on stage – the image more than the man.

"She was just too shallow, that daughter of mine. She was too selfish to appreciate him really. Still ran around, still used him. He would come and sit down on my back step, cry to me 'bout Sheena, my own daughter, and how she was playing with his feelings. I was the first one he told when he got the offer to play on that cruise ship, and I was the one who encouraged him to go." Zahara could tell Granny Linda still felt guilty over that.

"He was a good man. And for his own sanity, I encouraged him to go and not look back…and he took me at my word."

She suddenly had this image of her father, a guitar slung across his back, travelling from port to port. She could see how it would be hard to know where he'd settled, eventually, with the whole world at his feet.

"She found out she was wi' chile not long after he left," Granny Linda went on, pulling Zahara's thoughts back to the dark room and darker memories. "She didn't even know if you were his really until you were born," Granny Linda said bitterly. "But when I saw you, I knew. You are the spit of him, and when you wouldn't leave that damned guitar alone, there was no denying you took after him."

She was startled by this. She'd always thought she was a bad copy of her mother, could it be that she was actually a good copy of her father?

"Did she ever tell him?"

"Couldn't find him. He'd taken my advice to heart. And she didn't even know that I was the one who'd betrayed her; though maybe she suspected because she just got worse after he left. I think we broke her heart, both Sylvester and I." There was a catch in Granny Linda's voice as she made this last confession.

Zahara was shocked. So her grandmother had been carrying around her guilt all these years?

"It's not your fault," she said softly.

Granny Linda broke down and cried. Zahara felt her whole world tilt dangerously. Granny Linda was the rock that her life rested on. Now it was like the rock had given away, as though someone had taken a jack-hammer to it, sending shards scattering. She didn't know what to do, so she did the only thing she could. She put her arms around grandmother and held on.

Chapter 22

He startled, wondering what had pulled him out of his sleep. He shook off the dregs of his dream, something about dreadlocked spiders. He looked around blearily in the dim light, saw his cell dancing on his desk, next to his laptop. He reached across, picked it up.

It was a text from Zahara.

Not sibs

He laughed out loud at that. His life felt like a weird country and western song, what if my girlfriend was my sister, or something. Maybe he should write that. Yeah, that'd be kind of hype, or maybe just weird.

tld u he texted back.

They were about three hours into practice when Kong's mother showed up. After a few words with Mr. Perry, Mrs. Jean-Baptiste called them together for a prayer. Apparently, her contribution to the production was to be its official Prayer Warrior. Kong looked like he wanted to sink into the floor; everyone else looked like they wanted to laugh. But at a stern look from Mr. Perry they'd all shuffled to form a circle.

And she began, "Hold hands. Heavenly Father, I ask you to look down on these young people. Give them courage, Father, and focus, Father, and though they glorifying that liard, tiefing, no good Anansi, recognize the work that they put in, Father, and make them bruk leg but nuh fall down."

There were coughs and suppressed giggles as all the members of the production stood on the stage, two circles deep, holding hands. Shaka smiled. There would be no end of teasing Kong for this.

Would serve him right for his lippy ways.

He glanced at Kong, who was glaring at his mother as she continued praying. She was really getting into it, her voice dipping and diving, punctuating every prayerful request with more and more 'Fathers.'

Truth was they needed prayer. In the last few days the whole play had felt like it was falling apart. People were forgetting their lines, missing their cues… it was as if they were in the throes of a collective meltdown. They were panicking and right on time Kong's mother arrived and did her church mama thing.

"Okay," Mr. Perry said softly, when the circle broke up. "Take five then meet back in ten."

He smiled. That was Mr. Perry's standard wise-crack about so-called "Antigua time." Their teacher hadn't been much for joking in the past few days, so it was good to see him relaxed again.

They splintered off, most of them descending on the snacks provided each night now by Zahara's grandmother, as well as other parents who were chipping in. Tonight, someone had made baked plantain balls stuffed with cheese.

"Put cheese inna anything an' 'e bang good," Big Head declared, stuffing two at once into his mouth.

"Disgusting," Nicola said, turning away, nibbling on a piece of banana bread.

Shaka grabbed Zahara's hand to pull her outside. Kong saw them and started humming Promise's "Carnival Nookie" song.

"Yeah, yeah," Shaka teased. "Pray for me…no, wait, your mommy already did that." *That* shut Kong up, *brap!*

"So?" he said when they were alone.

"So," she said.

"So, I can't believe you actually asked her," he said.

"Well, I didn't ask her if we were related; she doesn't even know you."

Ouch.

"What you vex 'bout? Ent you get the answer you want?" he snapped.

She huffed. "It's complicated."

He waited but she didn't say anything else. Just then, Mr. Perry called them back together. Practice went pretty well after that. They actually managed a complete run-through in close to running time with only a few tweaks here and there. Maybe they could finally get around to practicing the flash mob routine they'd been planning to promote the show.

"Now we cooking with gas," Mr. Perry declared and everyone whooped. They were getting there, and not a moment too soon. It was two days before opening night.

He didn't get a chance to talk to her again during practice. He'd gotten good at reading her though, especially

199

since Mr. Perry had encouraged him to try to see things from her perspective during their impromptu boxing lesson.

He knew she wasn't mad at him, that she was still processing everything. He was too, and like him, she probably didn't know how she felt about any of it.

He just wished she'd talk to him instead of going into these moods though. He might understand it, but it was still irritating and it wasn't fair, not when he was an open book to her. He didn't like how one-sided it felt, like he was putting something on the line she wasn't.

He'd worked himself down to a brood of his own by the time his phone indicated it had an incoming text.

He, Pappy, and his mother were eating the rice pudding his grandfather had picked up from one of the night-time street vendors on the way home. Even his love of the black, spicy, meat and rice stuffed favourite couldn't lift him out of his funk. His mother teased him about girl troubles, while Pappy, usually the one doing the teasing, just watched him, no doubt figuring his mood had something to do with recent revelations. He wouldn't be wrong.

He perked up and excused himself when he saw the text.

His grandfather said "go 'head" while his mother warned with a smile, already eyeing his plate, that she couldn't guarantee that the rest of his rice pudding would be there when he returned.

He called from his room. She answered right away.

"You ready to talk to me now?" he asked without preamble.

"I don't know if I can," she admitted.

Irritation flared in him again. He'd told her everything Pappy had said, right away. She had no business holding out on him.

"I love you," she said.

Wow.

"What?"

"I love you," she repeated, sounding just as surprised to be saying it as he was to be hearing it.

He felt both thrilled and scared, felt like his heart was about to jump out of his mouth into the phone. It was the weirdest feeling, caused his breath to hitch.

"You don't have to say it back," she said. But she sounded let down, and who could blame her. Who went silent when somebody said, "I love you?" Who would have thought she'd be the first to say it? And why was he still standing there like a fooly-booly with no words?

"No, I was just thinking 'bout when we first met," he said, finally, and it was sort of true, because their entire relationship was flashing through his mind. "You wouldn't even give me the time o' day."

"I remember," she said.

"That girl would be shocked."

Why was he teasing at a time like this? Why was he the one suddenly struggling to put his feelings on the line? He could hear Kong in the back of his head going, "man up, man."

She laughed a bit nervously, said, "I'm still me."

And she was.

"Yes, you are," he said. "Just more you, you know. And mi lub you too."

She released a breath, giggled.

"Way to leave a girl hanging."

"Well, you nearly give me wan heart attack," he said. "Had to catch my breath."

"I love you," she said.

"I love you," he responded.

She told him everything then, everything; and he told her he was sorry about her father, the possibility of her never knowing who he was.

She admitted that that part was rough. It wasn't like him and his father. All now, he still didn't long for him or the idea of him, but with her, the reality of a father had just been placed in her head and at the same time the uncertainty of ever knowing him. That must be rough.

"You still have your Granny Linda," he said.

"Yeah, I do," she agreed, but she sounded wistful, and they both knew that she and her granny might be in a better place but everything would still take time. It's what his mother always said, "stop being in such a rush, everything take time." He wondered, now, though, if she had ever properly moved on. She'd never been with another man that he knew of, that wasn't no kind of way to live. He'd always taken it for granted but now he found himself wondering.

Now he was feeling wistful.

He defaulted to humour.

"Wha'ever else, you have me and me have you. Me na know 'bout them and them na know 'bout we, but tight like Squeeze ah so arwe be... solid as a rock."

He rapped his own lyrics over two familiar melodies.

She laughed. "I think you have your genres, and your generations mixed up."

He loved that she knew right away that he was sampling from Usher and Alicia, and Ashford and

Simpson. Some other girl might have just said, "huh?" But for both of them, their music knowledge was so deep; it bonded them. Yeah, music was guaranteed to pull both of them out of a funk.

He laughed, "Whatever. I'm like Yeezus, I'm on a different level, you all don't even know."

"Pappyshow," she teased.

"Present, please," he quipped back.

And they talked like that until his mother knocked to tell him it was "time enough" for him to come off the phone and go to sleep. His battery was almost dead anyway. He waited for his mother to walk away before saying one final "love you" and hanging up.

Chapter 23

Tempers were fraying. The curtain call was supposed to be done in dance and they were just learning the moves the night before opening night. Everyone was on edge, especially the non-dancers like Zahara.

On top of that, they were going to promote the show by performing it flash mob-style in Market Square the following morning...Saturday morning... Market day.

It was already late and they still hadn't got it. *She* still hadn't gotten it and Mr. Perry had just announced that they weren't leaving the theatre until they did.

"Boss, you manage fu find the one black gyal wid no rhythm," Kong joked.

Shaka shot him a glare and reached for her hand.

"Come on," he coaxed. "You'll get it, nuh worry."

"Yeah, you will," Nicola said, stepping to the other side of her.

Nicola did the shoulder shake, like a shrug; she added the neck snap, the pumping of the chest, like a heartbeat, and the sharp left to right motion of the hips. And that's where she lost Zahara. It was like trying to tap your head and rub your belly at the same time, while holding your breath and trying to work out an algebra problem; her brain got confused.

"Come," Shaka said, doing the rhythmic shrugging motion, just that. She followed suit. But then, just as she started to get that, Nicola's hands settled on her hips from behind, rocking with her, side to side, side to side. And just as she started to feel like "yes, yes, me hab um", Nicola and Shaka let go. She felt like a child learning to ride a bicycle without training wheels. Not that she'd ever learned to ride a bike but it's what she imagined that would feel like.

She didn't give in to the disorientation though. She kept moving.

"I got it!" she said, and not even the words distracted her. Her body suddenly knew what to do.

"Okay, now add the hop," Shaka said… and it all fell apart again.

She blamed Mr. Samuel. He'd insisted on taking charge of the curtain call and had waited to the last minute to drill them. After talking their ears off.

"Cause you see in Africa, dance is not just this wiggle up thing," he said shaking his body. "Dance is conversation between man and man, man and woman, man and nature, man and God. Is affirmation, is mourning, is celebration. It infuse all areas of life. In Africa, baby born, they have a dance for that. Girl wan' let boy know she interested? There's a dance for that. Man and woman marry, or maybe smadee dead? It have dance there for all that too. And you know what? You already know um because ah dey all ah arwe come from. So come, get up, let's dance!"

The girl playing Anansi's mother griped, "He spend the whole summer ah sleep an' now wan' teach man fu dance."

Mr. Samuel led them through the steps, talking as he demonstrated.

"Now, story done, so we celebrating. Remember to smile and make that smile come all through your big toe." He demonstrated the fast-shrug, chest-flex, hip-sway action. "This is Ethiopian, East Africa, lots of shoulder and neck action, you see? Like that."

"Isn't Anansi from West Africa?" Zahara snarked.

She didn't mean to be rude but, if he was going to teach them such complicated movements, he should have started earlier.

"We getting there," Mr. Samuel said. "This is just the beginning." The choreographer was now pounding his stick on the wooden floor of the stage. "Okay, break time over," he said. "From the top!"

Yup, she definitely wanted to cry.

The next morning, she stood in the middle of Market Square. Her eyes burned from lack of sleep and her body felt jittery. They'd practiced into the early hours of the morning, leaving only enough time to go home, freshen up, and grab a quick breakfast, before meeting at the square at mid-morning.

She was nervous. But last night she'd danced until her brain shut down and muscle memory took over, so she felt she wouldn't totally embarrass the group. Still, she had enough resentment left in her to give Dan and Kong the stink eye as she took her place with the other dancers. As the drummers, they were the only people who hadn't had to learn the stupid dance.

"Z, me never know you have so much wire in yuh waist," Kong had teased during rehearsals.

Their drums for the occasion were only white plastic buckets, turned upside down; but when they started beating them—Kong with his hands, Dan with his sticks—it sure sounded like music.

Nicola and Shaka, dressed in the same black t-shirt and jeans they all wore, started things off.

Shoulder-shrug, chest-pump, hip-sway, hop.

Shoulder-shrug, chest-pump, hip-sway, hop.

Zahara's body tensed up in anticipation of her cue, heart somewhat eased by the anonymity provided by the spider masks that they wore.

Shaka whipped off his mask and initiated the electric slide. Everyone quickly fell into step, even her. Some of the onlookers joined in. She was stepping on toes a bit as she tried to figure it out but everyone seemed to be having fun.

Upfront, Shaka was moving so fluidly it was like he was boneless and as he spun she saw, too, that he had a big grin on his face. Clearly, the nerves he'd confessed to feeling were gone. She hadn't been worried. He was born for this.

Vendors and shoppers alike had stopped what they were doing to watch, cars had slowed in the street nearby. It was the most exciting thing she'd ever been a part of, the most attention she'd ever had on herself at one time. The crowd whooped and applauded when they stopped. She could get used to this.

Having grabbed the crowd's attention and fed off of their enthusiastic response, it wasn't hard to chat up people and sell tickets. She could hardly wait for the night's performance. And looking around at everyone, including Shaka who caught her eye with a wink, she could see she wasn't the only one.

Chapter 24

He and Zahara stopped by the radio station afterwards. They were almost sleepwalking by that point but Diva had asked him to come.

"Ah wha' mek you look so?" Diva joked when she saw him. He gave her the finger and she grabbed it and twisted. "Respect your elders," she said, before pulling him into a hug. "Stranger," she chastised, mildly.

"I know," he said. "But these rehearsals, jack."

"Hmm," Diva said. Then she switched her attention to Zahara. "So, she's the one."

"She's the one," he agreed.

Zahara turned a nice shade of plum.

The radio DJ stuck out her hand; Zahara shook it.

"I taught this one everything he know 'bout music," Diva said.

He rolled his eyes at that.

"Well, you did a good job," Zahara said, finding her tongue.

"So, you guys have a minute? Folks been calling in 'bout your song. I thought you could come on air and talk about it little bit," Diva said. She was already moving down the hall toward the room with the 'on air' sign above the door. Shaka looked at Zahara and shrugged. They were dead on their feet but at the same time couldn't pass up the impromptu opportunity to talk about their song.

He took Zahara's hand and followed Diva to the smaller room, a familiar room with its controls and mics; signed artiste posters on the wall and stacks of music CDs. Most of what Diva needed would be on the computer but she was also known for spinning unusual and forgotten tunes pulled from the pile within arms' reach. He and Zahara settled in across from her.

He let go of her hand to help her with her headphones. Diva raised a brow but didn't say anything, which he was glad for. Her humour could be a bit much to take at times. He didn't want to spook Zahara, though she wasn't quite so spookable these days.

He observed as Diva did her thing, pressing keys and buttons before going on air.

"You na see your nail an' dem waan cut, don't know how you get anything done," he teased. Brightly coloured nails that looked like the claws on a bird of prey were another Diva signature.

"The better to scraaarp you up with," Diva said, stretching forward to flick playfully at his face causing him to lurch back. She was laughing as she adjusted the mics, settled her headphones over her head, then asked, "Aryuh ready?"

"We can't stay long," Shaka reminded her. "We been up all night…"

"T-M-I," Diva interrupted.

"Practicing," he continued, rolling his eyes.

"Oh, is *that* what they calling it these days," Diva joked. She could be so inappropriate sometimes. It was one of the things that had appealed to him as a kid in an adult world, when his mom had forced him to start going to the station to "learn a trade." Now, he was conscious of Zahara, quiet beside him, and quickly pressed on before Diva had chance to embarrass him again.

"We just did a performance at Market Square and we have to be at the theatre for six this evening."

"Look at you, all grown up and ting," Diva teased. And then just as she pressed the button to go live, taking over from the computer program that had been running the station in her absence, her demeanour changed and she became the professional all of Antigua and Barbuda knew her to be.

"Hey, this is Diva, you all!" she said. "And the Prodigal Son has found his way home. Zulu, say something to the people."

He started at the old name. He hadn't heard it in so long, his friends having adjusted surprisingly quickly to using Shaka after he started calling himself that.

"Actually, it's Shaka these days," he said into the mic.

"But see ya, okay Shaka Zulu," Diva replied. And he felt his cheeks burn.

But then Zahara piped up, "A great warrior."

Diva laughed her belly full. "That he was, gi' dem Brits ah thorough ra…" and she used one of the sound effects she kept on hand to drown out the expletive.

Next to him, Zahara laughed.

"Ladies and gentlemen, that saucy minx is Shaka Z's lady. Lady, tell them who you be."

"Hi, I'm Zahara."

And in the dead air that followed, Diva's voice teased, "Oh Gad, jack, stop talking off mi ear, gi' somebody else a chance fu get a word in, jack."

214

He and Zahara cracked up, and just like that Diva had put them both at ease. For the next five minutes they talked about the production. Then Diva went all out urging listeners to support the production.

"Aryuh find money fu go ah Robot City every night ah Carnival, not to mention every heels-too-expensive, blue-jeans-too-tight fête, so mek sure aryuh go support the young people an' dem. The two ah dem in here looking like extras offa de Walking Dead so you know dem work hard…" Diva skilfully segued to a background fadeout of Whitney Houston singing the first verse of "The Greatest Love of All."

Next, they talked about music.

"You hear wha' me say people, girlfriend play guitar, write song and ting. As for the rest ah yuh, I been reading some ah the headlines today-self, an' me ha fu wonder, what are *you* about?"

Zahara blushed at that.

"Hey, guitar girl," Diva prodded. "Melissa Ethridge or Joan Jett?"

"Nancy Wilson," Zahara replied without missing a beat.

Shaka felt a surge of pride. And Diva was on point immediately cycling through "Alone," everybody's favourite song from the Heart sisters.

215

"Alright, alright… Joni Mitchell or Bonnie Raitt?" Diva asked next, and he knew his old mentor was testing Zahara to see if she was worthy of him. He could have told her how encyclopaedic his girl's knowledge of music was, but some people had to learn the hard way. He sat back with a smirk as Zahara stepped up to the challenge like a champ.

"Elizabeth Cotten," she said. And Diva was stumped.

Thanks to Zahara, he actually knew who Cotten was; Zahara had pulled up a Smithsonian recording of Cotton playing "Going Down the Road Feeling Bad" on YouTube.

"She's a lefty, but she plays a right-handed guitar," Zahara had said to him, her inner music nerd coming out. "You know how hard that is? That means she has to play the melody with her thumb and the bass with her fingers. Come on now; that's rock 'n roll!"

He remembered laughing then and teasing her, "Okay, Pink."

"Alright, alright," Diva responded with something like respect in her voice.

They talked about the song, "Melanin."

"So much cleverer than 'Dem ah bleach,' am I right folks? No offence, Nardo."

She played his song; he still couldn't believe something he'd written was actually on the radio. Perks of living in a country so small, he supposed. Everybody knew somebody, who knew somebody else who had the key to the door you needed to get through. It could be a pain, but when it worked, it worked.

"How'd this come about?" Diva asked.

"I had a school project," Zahara began.

"I was helping her with that," Shaka interjected.

"Yeah, it was how he got me involved in the theatre group."

"Took some arm twisting," he added and Zahara screwed up her face at him.

"Anyway, we were trying different things. I was doing a lot of research and we'd talk about it, about black people and the self-hate that has us tearing up our skin to look white, and just ending up looking freakish. We were trying to understand where that all comes from."

"It's a real issue isn't it?" Diva said. "When are we going to get with the programme?"

"You know what though?" Zahara said, warming to the subject. "I don't judge. I mean, think about it. We were enslaved for like, hundreds of years, right. In the case of Antigua, it's been less than two hundred years since black people been legally free, and a hundred-and-eighty of those years we were still ruled by colonial masters, you know. It seem slow but the fact that we even having this conversation, the fact that this song so popular, says to me that we're moving forward."

"Yes, yes, baby steps," Diva agreed. She grinned at him. "Shaka, you sure you smart enough for this one? She brain big bad."

"That good, she can teach me," he replied.

"We teach each other," Zahara said.

And while he appreciated that, he knew he could never match her depth and passion. She was the most special girl he'd ever known, and, no, he wasn't biased at all.

He walked her to her door, a first, and she asked him to wait. She went in and after a while, came back out with Granny Linda

Zahara's grandmother was wearing a faded and frayed jean skirt, and an old t-shirt damp with sweat, probably from the heat in the kitchen where she'd likely been cooking up treats for their food station later. He hoped. They'd all fallen in love with her cooking.

He observed as well that she wore her slippers with socks like Pappy sometimes did around the house, her hair pulled back from her face but not quite tamed, and her smile confused. She was pretty like Zahara. Somehow he hadn't expected that, with all the horror stories he'd heard. He hadn't really been checking for it the other night; he'd been too shocked to see her and Pappy embracing. They said if you want to see how a girl was going to look when she get older, look at her mother; Granny Linda was not Zahara's mother but close enough. Socks and slippers aside, his girl was going to age well.

"This is Mark Durante," Zahara said. "He goes by Shaka."

Granny Linda looked him up and down. He took his cue from Zahara and waited.

"Durante," Granny Linda said, finally. "Who your people?"

"My mother is Wendy Commodore," he said.

"Commodore, Commodore…"

"Yes, Errol Commodore is my grandfather."

"So your father is …"

"*Was* Watty Durante, yes."

He didn't even dip his eyes when he said it. He wasn't ashamed of who he was. And Zahara was showing him that she wasn't ashamed to claim him, even with all his baggage. This was a girl who got licks for sneaking out just weeks ago. He knew this step wasn't easy for her. He was proud of her and was going to be the kind of boyfriend she could be proud of too. So, let Granny Linda bring it, he could take it.

She looked at him like she was trying to read him. She didn't say anything further, just looked. And he stood up to her scrutiny; didn't even squirm.

He wondered what she saw beyond his black t-shirt, black jeans, and black skin. Did she see his father, the man who had taken her daughter from her? Did she see trouble? Everything he knew about her said she was the type who would have preferred Zahara not even look at a boy, any boy, until she was done with school, much less the son of the man who had taken her daughter from her. Nothing he could do about that except be himself. Besides, she should know by now the kind of girl she'd raised; should know that Zahara had a good head on her shoulders. He'd seen that even before she had talked to him.

"Hmm, I think I smell my bakes burning," was all Granny said before turning and walking back inside.

"Well that went better than I hoped," Zahara commented.

"Really?" he said. "'Cause I couldn't tell."

"Oh, believe me, if she didn't want me seeing you or bringing you around, she'd ah said so. She don't mince words."

"Oh."

A few hours later, Shaka walked to the theatre with his Crew a little more subdued than usual.

"Hey," Kong said. "Me hear you an' you girl 'pon Diva show earlier."

"Yeah, she ambush arwe," he responded.

"Me lub how Diva handle the nincompoop that call een an' talk 'bout bleaching ah just one choice, an' slavery deep in the past," Kong continued.

"Brethren me see you ah read from the Kartel Bible, but we don have time for them kinda vibes," Monkey quoted Diva verbatim.

"Yeah, Diva just wicked," Accident said.

"Some ah dem smadee that ah call in radio station nuh ha' the sense God gi' one fowl," said Big Head.

"You tell one fowl 'shoo shoo' an' two seconds later 'e right back again," they all quoted in unison. That was from the Pappy bible of why children can't be trusted not to chop off their own foot. The saying had

221

stopped being funny to Kong after he almost lost his foot, though the mishap had kind of proven Pappy's point.

"Chupid ah fart!" Kong added, drawing his attention back, as they continued along the familiar route.

As they approached the end of the route Shaka found himself feeling sentimental, his mind casting back to when he'd first met them. Big Head, the boy with the head too big for his body; Monkey, the boy who was a born copycat, Scaly, the boy with the ashy feet from lack of lotion; Accident, the boy who was then always tripping over his own feet and falling down; and the boy who would become Kong, chattier than anybody he had ever met before or since.

He remembered how his mother had walked with him, holding his hand, the first week of primary school. She'd taken the week off work so she could take those walks with him, lecturing him as they went along about which route was safe to take, which streets she'd better not hear he'd been on, and what time he'd better be home by. He followed the rules to the letter at first. Then he'd met the Lion Crew, the group coming together mostly because they lived roughly in the same direction, and the walk home had started taking a little longer.

When he said Lion Crew for life, he meant it. His boys had been there through everything, and now, thinking about it, he wondered if any of them would even have found themselves at an audition for a play if it hadn't been for that simple fact. They had each other's backs. If one of the boys had developed an interest in cricket, he might have been a budding Viv Richards instead of a budding Ne-Yo. And, thank God for that, he thought smiling to himself. Nothing against Sir Viv; the man was cool for an older dude, but he just loved music too much.

"Ah wha' you ah grin so fa," Kong said, cuffing him. "Zahara na here nuh, an' me nuh skin teet' wit' no man."

"Homophobe," he said.

"Hey, to each his own," his friend said, the picture of innocence. "And I'll take mine like Kentucky with breasts and thighs, thank you very much."

"What no *bounce batty*," Monkey said, singing the last two words of the K. Lee soca song.

Shaka shook his head and rolled his eyes. "You guys..."

"Oh, look at him, he's so sensitive." Kong teased and as if on cue, Monkey sang the old song "Sensitivity."

They teased each other all the way to the theatre.

223

They heard the noise before they even got backstage. Shaka frowned.

"That's Zahara."

He rushed forward and came upon Zahara in the midst of a heated confrontation with Dan the Man.

"It's mine!" Dan was saying, pulling on one end of those mesh shirts they were making the band wear.

"No, it's not, it's mine!" Zahara retorted, pulling on the other end.

Wha' this, primary school? Where the adult an' dem? Shaka wondered.

"Wha' goin' on?" he demanded, deciding to be the adult in the room while everyone else stood around, either gaping silently or egging the combatants on.

"He lost his shirt and now wants to act like he don know this is mine," Zahara said.

"It *is* mine!"

"No, it's not. See? It has the rip in the shoulder."

"Because you just ripped it just now when you were pulling on it!" Dan shouted back.

"Liar!"

"What's the big deal?" Shaka interrupted. "Wear another shirt."

He couldn't believe this stupidness was what they were fighting for.

"There is no other shirt," Dan said through gritted teeth.

"So wear the shirt you have on." Shaka could really care less what the other boy wore.

"And be the odd man out?" Dan said incredulously.

Are we really having this conversation? Shaka thought.

"So I'm supposed to be the odd girl out because you were too careless to keep track of your clothes?" Zahara said, not giving any ground.

"Well, you already odd, it won't be much of a stretch," Dan said.

Next thing he knew, Kong was in Dan's face. "Watch who you calling names, Dan the Man."

Kong had lived up to his name, packing on a lot of weight over the years. That plus his height made for an imposing presence. The other boy let go of the shirt and stepped back. Shaka stepped forward and placed a hand on his friend's chest, patting slightly. Kong relaxed.

"Okay," he said, turning back toward Dan and Zahara. "Everybody good? Because seriously, guys, we have a play to do…in like two hours."

"I still don't have no shirt," Dan said sullenly.

Shaka tried not to laugh but, seriously, the drummer looked and sounded about five years old.

225

"Well, call your nanny and have her drop it off for you nuh." He couldn't resist the nanny dig. He was trying to make peace but he never said he was a saint.

The other kids giggled and Dan looked even more embarrassed as he confessed, "I don't know where it is."

Nicola stepped forward then. "It's cool," she said. "We'll figure something out."

Dan looked unconvinced even as his girlfriend, stepping up to her leadership role as a principle cast member, looked around for inspiration. Nicola's eyes landed on Shaka and she made grabby hands in his direction.

"Give me that."

"What?" he asked, stepping back.

"Hey, your girl got her shirt, now give me the blasted necklace," Nicola demanded.

"Hey!" This from both him and Zahara.

"Sorry, Z," said Nicola.

But she was still making grabby hands at him and advancing. He had no idea what she was after and only stopped retreating when his butt hit the edge of the make-up station. Nicola reached up, pushed the top of his head down with one hand, lifted his necklace off with the other. It was the one with the ites, gold, and green beads and the Africa pendant with Bob Marley's face that hung down to about mid-stomach. She gave it to Dan.

"Put that on," she commanded. Then she snatched Scaly's orange mirrored sunglasses, perched harmlessly atop his head. "And that," she added. "Take off the shirt first, idiot," she ordered Dan. "You're right; the shirt would stand out and not in a good way."

Dan opened his mouth to protest.

"Take off the shirt," Nicola repeated, her tone not leaving room for argument.

Dan took his shirt off. It wasn't a pretty sight. He wasn't fat-fat, but he hadn't lost his baby softness either. There was snickering but Nicola glared and it quieted down. Dan put the necklace on, and the shades, clearly embarrassed.

"I have a black, crocheted waistcoat with fringe tassels that's too big for me," Nicola said, pulling out her cell. "I'll call my mom and tell her to bring it."

She was already punching numbers.

"You want me to wear a girl's vest?"

"It's either that or the belly." Nicola slapped Dan's belly. The drummer coloured even more, his mortification hard to hide with his fair complexion.

"It'll be fine," she said, when she got off the phone and saw him still standing there in nothing but

227

Joanne C. Hillhouse

shiny black pants, the necklace, and shades, his 'fro sticking out in all directions.

"You look hot," she said. "Very rock 'n roll."

Shaka rolled his eyes. So *that*'s where Zahara had picked up that expression.

Chapter 25

She had to admit, it was kind of cool seeing Kong step up to defend her honour like that.

She hadn't been sure initially that Shaka's boys even liked her. They'd eventually gotten used to having her around and she too had grown accustomed to them and their antics. But when he got up in Dan's face, Kong had declared that she was one of them; she was a part of the Lion Crew. She looked at them now—Accident, Monkey, Scaly, and Big Head with their masks sitting on their heads, lanky bodies encased in bodysuits that were, in her opinion, an improvement over the pants-down, boxers-out fashion they favoured. Kong pulled on Shaka's pretend locks causing the wig to slip every time he turned away and she felt a warm affection.

"Okay, chicks, time to leave the nest, it's show time!" Mr. Perry bellowed the last word, and if he didn't have everyone's attention before, he had it now.

She hoped there was no one front of house as yet. They were still about forty-five minutes from show time. Of course, for Antiguans, showing up a few minutes late was as good as being right on time. Mr. Perry had insisted that they were going to buck that trend though; the curtain would go up at the advertised time even if there was only one person in the theatre.

The idea of performing for just one person actually relaxed her a little. As a band member, she'd be down in an improvised music pit below the stage, in plain view of the audience, even when the curtain was drawn between acts. She was already nervous about that.

She pulled at the bustier as Mr. Perry directed them to hold hands. Kong groaned as his mother emerged as if from nowhere, to lead them in prayer. They all hung their heads and bit their lips, welcoming the prayer but fighting the urge to laugh at Kong's discomfort.

Since he was playing the djembe, Kong was dressed like the band, in satin and mesh and he'd dug up some dark shades from somewhere.

Was that a thing? Would she be the only one without sunglasses? She looked across at Ted. Yep, he was wearing them too, those shutter shades like Kanye wore.

"You see what you started," she told Nicola as they milled about the green room afterward. "All the musicians wearing shades except me."

Nicola laughed. "Ent you got the shirt, wha' you worried 'bout?" She gave her friend the stink eye.

They were standing side by side in front of the standing mirror in the backstage area curtained off for just the ladies.

"You look hot," Nicola said. "Legs for days."

The compliment made her want to cover them up, but she forced herself to look. She had to admit they made quite the pair. There she was in her rocker shorts, bustier-style sports bra and mesh vest, and, yes, legs for days in a rocking pair of boots. And, as was the case with the other band members, her kinks were sticking up in all directions, like she was Solange Knowles or somebody. But she still felt like herself, like it was her. She actually kind of liked what she saw, even if they were just playing dress-up.

Nicola was barefoot, and only came up as far as Zahara's shoulder but as usual she stood tall, the headwrap giving her a few more inches and framing her face in a way that was straight from the motherland.

"You look beautiful," Zahara told her.

Nicola rolled her eyes and looked down at her dress. "I look like my grandmother."

"Well, then she must be a very beautiful woman, because you are beautiful."

Nicola looked up again and their eyes met in the mirror. Nicola turned this way and that and finally smiled. "I am, aren't I?"

"You know it."

Just then a pair of arms slung around both their shoulders and Shaka's reflection joined theirs in the mirror. He was in full Anansi dress. For the opening he'd be wearing the 'superhero' suit and then he'd switch into a khaki pants and unbuttoned denim shirt with ripped sleeves. He'd be wearing his locs throughout.

"Watch the two of you all having the fellas falling to their knees," he said, doing just that, a graceful move she found herself admiring even as she swatted him on the back of his head.

"Should never have given you that book to read," she said. "Leave it to you to completely miss the point."

"Which book that?" Nicola asked.

"My Maya Angelou," she said.

"Deep stuff," he cut in. "And you are a phenomenal woman."

Nicola laughed. "Whaaaa, Zahara, all them lyrics for you one?"

She rolled her eyes and stalked off to join the band, their laughter following after her. She couldn't stop grinning.

Her mind leapfrogged from one thing to the next as she waited in the dim light for the band's cue.

She thought of Granny Linda somewhere out there in the full theatre, because, yes, they had a full theatre. She'd spotted familiar faces like her choir director, Pappy and, maybe, Shaka's mother just before the lights went down and while she hadn't seen Granny Linda, she had a feeling she was there, too. Something had opened up between them, it's why she'd felt emboldened, if not exactly comfortable, enough to bring Shaka to meet her.

She thought of the ghosts of her parents, because though one was living, presumably, and one was dead, they were both ghosts to her for all practical purposes. She didn't know if she thought of them as angels watching over her, but she had an awareness of them of late that she attributed to hearing their history, such as it was.

She thought of every long night, every stray tear, the friendships forged, the misunderstandings overcome this long summer of rehearsals, and had to smile to herself at where she'd ended up, in the orchestra of her first ever theatrical production. She felt happy and excited.

She knew, just behind the curtains, Shaka would be feeling much the same. He was no stranger to the stage but she knew he'd been nervous about this, nervous and yet at the same time giddy with excitement.

She pictured him bouncing on his toes as he waited for the curtain, the lights, the applause. No doubt one of his boys—not Kong who was settled behind his djembe—would be ribbing him as they did, and another would whisper encouragement – "mash um up." Monkey maybe, he was the type. And no doubt another of the boys would shush him setting off a round of quiet shoving before Shaka glared at them. Something else she'd become familiar with over the course of this summer, the rhythm of their interactions.

"Mash um up," Dan whispered to her, Ted, and Kong now, all grievances forgotten, and she almost laughed out loud at the way his words echoed her thoughts.

Just then the cue came and they all straightened and launched into their opening number.

Chapter 26

Shaka's mind shut down during the performance. It wasn't unusual for his mind to take a little vacation while his body went to work, moving through patterns drilled into it over weeks of repetition and practice, until he was nothing but movement and music.

The love of music that began with his introduction to the greats by Pappy had blossomed into something that felt as much a part of him as his arms, his legs, his beating heart.

He couldn't explain it if he tried, and he couldn't live without it even if he wanted to. He lived for those moments, for giving his whole body over to the dance.

In a way, he was more like the Granny character in Bryan's book than the Anansi character. After all she was the one who for the longest while, even when she knew what the trickster was up to, kept getting seduced by the music. It was like that Claudette Peter's song said, there was 'something' in the music.

He felt it as soon as the lights came up and the band struck up.

It was inevitable that he wouldn't remember anything from the performance. He never did. It was Pappy who would fill him in later in between telling him how proud he was of him.

"Always knew you had it in you."

Pappy, in that later conversation, would uncharacteristically, flatter him with comparisons to Fred Astaire, Gene Kelly, James Brown, Michael Jackson, Rex Nettleford, even Alvin Ailey, Gregory Hines, and Mikhail Baryshnikov—"Bwoy me na in know you know ballet."

He knew it was exaggeration but still the references to those men who'd made life of their art would get him thinking that maybe he could make something of this mix of things that he did. Maybe he wouldn't someday have to give up music for a soul sucking nine-to-five.

"You think I could do it for real like for real for real," he'd say to Pappy. And Pappy, without missing a beat, would respond, "Bwoy, what ah been telling you all along? You determine who you be, what you can do in this world."

He wouldn't know it while twirling Nicola as Anansi led Granny in a merry dance, but his performance, his and the other actors, Zahara's music, all of it, that night also narrowed the gaping distance between two long ago friends. It was his favourite story that Pappy would share from the night, simply because he liked knowing that what they did moved people. Pappy and Granny Linda had danced in the aisles. Now, *that* he would like to have seen.

"I was surprised to see her to tell you the truth. Seemed like she'd retreated from the world, you know, and from what little I pick up from you, she real strict with that girl so, yeah, I wasn't expecting her. Is why I hadn't seen her in so long, she didn't go no-where, like she been in mourning all this time. But, come a time in life, a little light peep through and you have to punch your way out of the grave you build for yourself or get buried alive. I was there once, after your tanty died. Maybe more recent than that. But the Lin I saw the night of you-all show, bwoy she was a woman coming back to life.

"Took me a while to even realize she was there, with the way you landed on that stage like a human sized spider, contorting yourself this way and that, moving in ways a human body shouldn't be able to. Bwoy, you were the shit, I tell you."

That was a first, Pappy forgetting himself and cursing during conversation with him like he was one of the guys down by the taxi stand.

"It wasn't 'til your girl did that guitar solo and I heard that intake of breath and her name—'Zahara!'—that I realized someone was sitting on the aisle floor right next to my chair, right there so-so in her nice dress and heels. The place was pack, you hear. I thought about offering her my seat when I looked over and catch a hint of her profile, but thought better of it when I remember your mother was sitting on the other side of me.

"But after that it was like we were watching the show together, every leap, every laugh, both of us shaking our leg and feeling the pull of the music, old time music – a likkle Short Shirt, a likkle Obsti, some Sparrow, maybe somewhat, some Latumba, Hitman – mix in with the rackachaca so that we sorta remember it but hearing something new same time. More than anybody in that audience, we had a connection. Because of our history, yes, but because of the two ah you, you and that girl, the two good things to come outa all this mess, both up there doing your thing, making us proud. I get emotional, ah don' mind telling you, my heart swell up, my eyes well up, and when I look 'cross like I see everything I was feeling on her face too, even in the dim light. And she look 'cross at me and smile same way like she was feeling it too. All kind of mixed up feelings.

"Before we know it we were up and dancing, don't care ah damn 'bout who around and wha' dem ha fu say, an' before long like they catch the fever, ah so we jam, ah so we jook, ah so we dip, age ha fu make way for music. Like Swallow sing, 'the music too sweet!'"

Pappy had laughed at that point in the re-telling and Shaka had a high time picturing it. Had a hard time believing that he had been a part of creating it. It was a bigger response than they'd ever gotten at the high school fêtes. It was more special but comparable only to their night on the big stage at Carnival City. *Two memorable performances in one amazing summer.* Reliving it, even second hand, later, through his grandfather's eyes, he would feel it and also see it for the first time.

Shaka would remember that when the em-cee encouraged the crowd near the end to get up and dance, someone shouted, "We done start," and all of them on the stage laughed. Little did he know then that Pappy and Granny Linda were among the people they could see dancing in the aisles as the lights went up for the curtain call.

Zahara had squeezed in next to him, though they were in different sections. Both of them were wet with sweat like it was J'ouvert morning or something; shoulders shaking, hips swaying, hopping. He wasn't ashamed to admit to himself that some of the water running down his face was tears. The Crew would have probably made fun of him if they knew, but he could relate to Pappy and Granny Linda on that.

Pappy's story had an epilogue.

"She and your mother spoke. Wasn't planned but when Wendy get up and me and Lin was still dancing, it was unavoidable. Tell the truth we were both too happy right then to be nervous. I didn't forget the care of my brain and tell her everything, but I did tell her that Lin was Zahara's grandmother, and Lin, of course, realized who she was. But not even that awkwardness could kill the mood."

Yeah, though he wouldn't get all those details until later, in conversation with his grandfather, his body recalled well enough the high of performing that night. He figured it would have taken a lot to bring any of them down.

His brain had kicked back into gear and he could rely on his own memories enough to remember how pumped up they still were when they hit backstage.

"We killed it!" he screamed and everybody joined in, whooping it up. There was hugging and kissing, and, when he found Zahara, there was more kissing.

Some of the performers descended on the food which had been taunting them with its aromas all night. Others began to change out of their clothes and make-up, but really, they were all still so full of adrenaline, they didn't know what to do with themselves. Mr. Perry looked about done, his body starting to flag, his eyes wet. When he spoke, his voice was hoarse.

"I am so proud of all of you," he said, and not one of them rolled their eyes, or snickered, or made any kind of sarcastic remark. They all preened under the praise, soaking it up, knowing they'd earned it.

"We have something for you," Nicola said stepping forward. Mr. Perry looked surprised.

She pulled the thank-you card out of her bag. It had been her idea; she'd even bought it with her own money. She'd spent the past week or so haranguing them to sign it.

"And not with no generic crap either!" she'd insisted.

Mr. Perry held it like it was finery or something.

"Open it!" Nicola prodded him.

As he pried open the envelope, they all chanted, "Read it, read it, read it!"

With a little laugh and shake of his head, Mr. Perry did just that.

"Even though you gave the lead to that no talent boy Shac-Shac instead of me, I won't hold it against you. Thank you, Mr. Perry. I kind of like this drumming thing."

They all turned to look at Kong who, as expected, only smirked.

"Thank you, Mr. Perry, for teaching me that chemistry can be fun."

That had to be Nicola. Shaka had to admit, she wasn't half bad once she got her nose out of the air.

"Mr. Perry, consider this my IOU for an all-expenses-paid trip to Bora Bora when I make it big as a musician."

That was Dan.

"Mr. Perry, everybody always told me I was good at impersonations. Thanks for giving me a chance to be an original."

They had to rib Monkey a little bit about that, of course. But the truth was, he'd come into his own as a choreographer during his work on the production. Nobody in Antigua had seen anything like the Anansi dance on a theatre stage before. Shaka remembered how intimidated he'd been trying to take it on at first. He'd owned it tonight and he had Monkey to thank for that.

"Mr. Perry, can I keep the mask?"

Everybody looked around, wondering who'd written that. Then he caught sight of Big Head smirking.

"Well e na easy for me fu find subben fu fit fu me head," his friend joked. Everyone laughed with him, not at him, including Mr. Perry. Shaka hadn't seen the teacher look so at ease in a long time.

Mr. Perry continued to read the notes of gratitude and appreciation, including his own, and they lost track of time until one of the parents knocked on the door.

"How much longer?" It was Nicola's mom.

"Soon come," Mr. Perry replied and started to close the card. "Come on, kids, time to pack up."

Shaka frowned. He hadn't heard anything that sounded like Zahara.

"Wait, you have one more," he said. Mr. Perry opened the card and scanned it again.

He saw the glare Zahara sent him and only smiled in return. What was there to be embarrassed about? Besides, she couldn't stay mad at him for long, not tonight. The teacher found and read her sentiments.

"Mr. Perry, I owe you so much for helping me to come out of my shell."

"Zahara!" everyone chorused when he finished reading.

He was still looking at her, and she at him. She pursed her lips, blushed, shook her finger at him, and he just grinned even wider. He couldn't help it; he loved her and loved that she would be the one to go all deep then be embarrassed.

As for Mr. Perry, he pulled her into a hug, squeezing tight. Shaka could have been wrong, since no one commented on it, but he was pretty sure Mr. Perry was crying.

Chapter 27

She sat on her bed, her guitar across her lap, plucking idly, trying to calm her still thrumming body.

When she'd exited the theatre, she'd been surprised to find Granny Linda there waiting to take her home. She'd been wearing her costume still and half expected to be chastised for showing too much skin. But to her surprise, her grandmother had instead pulled her into a hug. She had realized then that Granny Linda had never hugged her before, not that she remembered. Maybe when she was a baby. *Everybody hugged babies, right?* Even people who didn't naturally show a lot of affection.

"Proud ah you, proud ah you," Granny Linda said before letting her go. As her grandmother walked away, Zahara had stood there. She waved dazedly at Nicola before the other girl hopped into her mother's vehicle and started when Shaka came up behind her and put an arm around her.

"Goodnight," Shaka said, with a wet kiss to her temple.

She turned. "Are you drunk?"

He giggled. "No, just high."

She did one of his patented head shake eye rolls, the kind of move he normally directed at Kong.

"Bye," she said, slipping away, conscious of her grandmother by the car waiting for her.

"Bye bye bye!" he sang before going off with Pappy and his mother.

It was quite possible she thought now, sitting on her bed, that *this* had been the best night of her life.

"It's all downhill from here," she sang, and with that thread of a beginning kept on singing, ad-libbing a song that she knew, even before she started, couldn't begin to capture everything this night had been.

Her phone vibrated. It was a text from Shaka.

U up?

She called him.

"Who could sleep?"

"It was wicked, right?" His voice sounded drowsy.

"Wicked," she agreed. He was silent and she wondered if he'd fallen asleep.

"It's weird," he said after a while. "I'm burned, but still hopped up, you know? Like me mi body ah say, 'tired now, sleep', but my brain rebelling, 'five more minutes, five more minutes'."

She laughed, softly. "I know what you mean."

"You were amazing tonight," he said. And it was sweet when his voice was all slurry like that.

"Look who's talking," she said.

"Hey, take the compliment," he pressed.

"You, too," she pushed back.

He laughed. "Mutual admiration society."

"We should get matching t-shirts."

He made a gagging sound.

"Let's not be that couple."

"Let's not," she agreed.

She spent the following morning at church. As usual, Granny Linda didn't go herself, but two nights of missed sleep was no excuse for her to scud. Still, as she made her way with her guitar slung as always over her shoulder, she was more buzzed than beat. Her mood lifted even more when Shaka met her at their usual spot by the lamppost at the bottom of the hill leading up to the church.

"Didn't think you'd be here today," she said.

"You think too much," he teased with a noisy yawn. His eyes were barely open, and his feet dragged.

When they got to the white, spherical building with the wooden cross on top, the place that had become her Sunday morning hell or sanctuary, depending on her mood, there was a surprise waiting for her. The youth choir members and band were gathered with Mr. Patrick, beaming at her like she'd just broken a world record or something, like she was Usain Bolt at the Olympics. They even had cake. *Where'd they get cake?*

Her growth as a musician while working on the production had spilled over to her performances with the church choir. The more she'd played, the more confidence she'd gained in her abilities, and the more she'd challenged herself to step out of her shell. Mr. Patrick had noticed and he'd been pleased to learn about her summer project. He'd even cut her some slack on a missed practice here and there, especially near the end when rehearsals for *The Dancing Granny* had all but consumed her life. She was surprised though to learn that the whole choir had come out to her performance the night before. And cake, they had cake!

Hopped up on sugar, it was hard to settle down for mass, even when Father Aames' droned on during the homily. It did make her nostalgic for Father Ellie, and eager to share everything with him.

"You can come Skype at my place," Shaka offered.

She didn't think twice before saying "Yes."

That's how she ended up at Shaka's place after church, instead of going straight home like Granny Linda would expect her to, skyping with Father Ellie in Shaka's room. Meanwhile, Shaka helped his mother, who hadn't been expecting company, prepare the Sunday morning breakfast.

Her boyfriend's room was its usual clutter; on the bed behind her, sat mountains of clothes that wouldn't get folded or hung up until his mother had yelled at him a few times.

She cleared a spot, and sat at the edge, setting her guitar next to her. She signed in to Skype hoping Father Ellie would be online. She wasn't sure what time mass ended at his parish in Jamaica but she knew, from previous conversations, that he usually blogged his sermons afterwards from his office.

She pressed video call and he responded immediately; his image, a more weathered version of the long-haired blue-eyed Jesus on the clock in her home room at school, coming into focus.

He'd changed from when she first met him, hair more white now than blonde, laugh lines wrinkling but not aging a forever boyish face. She remembered being envious of his blue eyes when she was a kid. She didn't feel that way anymore.

It seemed mass had only just ended. He was still in his vestments, like the White Jesus on the clock, not yet changed in to the off yellow shirt jacks he usually wore.

"Things went well, then?" he asked. She didn't ask how he knew; her cheeks were hurting, she was smiling so hard.

"Soooo well," she replied, and launched into the details.

"So let me hear some of it," Father Ellie said when she ran out of words.

Her eyebrows rose and her smile widened.

"Seriously? Now? Okay, wait a minute."

She picked up her guitar, set it across her lap, fingers immediately finding the chords for Granny and Anansi's theme. It felt so weird playing it for him, weirder than playing it for all those people last night.

But she was glad he'd asked. He was the first person who'd ever heard her play, the person who'd taken her interest in hearing him play for what it was: possibility. She wouldn't be who she was without him and she realized she'd never thanked him for that.

"That was a song I wrote," she said after she strummed the last chord.

He did a little silly clap that had her laughing out loud.

"I wish I could have been there to see it," he said. Then he added, surprise in his voice, "Look how far you come, eh?"

She didn't blame him for being surprised. She'd surprised herself in a million ways this summer.

"I have," she agreed.

"Good," he said.

And there wasn't much more to say after that. She logged off and sat there for a few minutes, thinking. After last night and now in this quiet moment with her mentor, she felt so tall, so full, so happy. She felt substantial, like somebody finally settling into her own skin in a way that made her realized she hadn't really been there before.

She'd not long signed off when Shaka came to the open door, still wearing his church clothes, and looking so different than he normally looked, in the blue tie and white shirt, jeans belted around his waist.

"Good chat?" he asked.

"Yeah," she said, still smiling. When she volunteered nothing more, he came to sit alongside her.

"Oh, let me show you something," he said and in the next minute he was tapping keys on the laptop.

Her mouth dropped open when "Melanin" started to play over images of Nicola of all people. The YouTube video was titled 'Melanin by Shaka, Zahara, Lion Cru, super producer Ted, and songstress Nic with additional vocals by Z'. The YouTube user who'd posted it was NubianNikki.

"Our first fan vid," Shaka said.

"Is it really a fan video if the person who posted it actually sang the hook?"

"Don't take this away from me, this is my first fan vid!" he said with mock seriousness.

She just shook her head.

"I can't believe she did this. When did she do this?"

"Found it last night, jus' before me call you. Was YouTubing 'cause I couldn't sleep."

She smacked his arm.

"How could you not tell me this?"

"Forgot," he said with a shrug.

"I can't believe she did this," she said, sounding like a broken record as he pressed replay.

The video wasn't really a video, just the track under images of Nicola from all ages of her life, beginning with one of her at about three years of age, wearing yellow shades with her hand on her thrust-out hip. Zahara shook her head. No one would guess looking at the girl in the pictures that she had any insecurities, but everyone did, didn't they? She turned to Shaka.

"I not doing the reality show thing again," she said, expecting a rebuttal. But he only nodded.

"Yeah, I know," he said. "Hard being a cutthroat reality show producer when you know the people an' dem."

"Yeah," she said.

"So wha' you goin' do?" he asked.

"I goin' do a write-up on what I learned while doing the research, working on the "Melanin" song, and taking part in the production, all in the week before school open," she said. "I'm calling it 'What I Did on My Summer Vacation'."

He laughed at that. Then his mother called them to breakfast.

Chapter 28

His mother was being weird. Well, the whole set up was weird. Them sitting down to breakfast like this, even on a Sunday when everyone was usually home, was weird. Usually Pappy ate in his chair, his mom grazed as she cooked, and he might eat in front of the TV, or reading or writing at the dining table, or in his room while using the computer.

This morning they were seated around the wooden dining table and he hadn't even heard Pappy complain about leaving his chair. Matching straw mats were set out along with the coasters with the picture of the St. John's Cathedral on them, collector's items his mom never let anyone use. The plastic fruit in the middle was set on one of her homemade doilies. She'd had him put it all in place before releasing him to check on Zahara.

Theirs was the usual Sunday morning fare of salt-fish, chop up, avocado pear, and cucumber sprinkled with salt and washed down with his favourite, soursop drink. He prayed that he wouldn't get white lip in front of his girl.

As he looked at the table, he had to admit he was impressed. His mother may not have been expecting company but as she'd told him when he'd asked if she'd mind Zahara staying for breakfast, "As my mammy told me, you always have to make sure you stretch you hand; you never know who might drop in."

As he'd helped her finish up and set the table, she'd told him how when she was growing up they didn't have much but there was always a little bit left in the pot for when Pappy brought home one of his liming buddies, or to send to bedridden Ms. Abraham up the road, or to offer one of the neighbourhood children whose parents didn't have enough.

"Is so people stay back then," she'd said. "Each one, help one. Not like now."

He'd tuned out half of what she said, to be honest. He'd heard about the good old days a million times and he was distracted, wondering if Zahara had reached Father Ellie. After all she'd told him about how the priest had been the one to introduce her to music and

256

nurture the talent he saw in her even when she didn't, he knew last night wouldn't be real until she'd spoken to him. He remembered how having Pappy, who'd opened the door to his love of music, squeeze his shoulder and tell him "Well done, bwoy" had meant everything.

She had spoken to Father Ellie, they were now seated over breakfast, and all was right with the world. Except his mother was being weird.

"You-all were real good last night," she said to Zahara.

"Thank you."

"Yeah, I like to see young people doing positive things."

"Yes, ma'am."

"It make you proud, you know."

"Yes, ma'am."

"I mean, obviously, I proud of this one here…but really of all of you."

"Thank you, ma'am."

It was like they'd stepped into 'Leave it to Beaver' or something. Polite conversation and on your Ps and Qs manners.

Weird.

Not that his mother wasn't polite and didn't have decorum but they were all usually so much more relaxed with each other. In the past, his mother had been relaxed enough to be her usual self with him—pick up your clothes! Come home straight!—even when the girl he most wanted to impress was right there.

"You've been a good influence on him."

"Uh, er."

It was clear she had something on her mind and Zahara seemed just as stumped as him. Shaka looked at Pappy, checking to see if he knew anything. But Pappy was too busy eating to care. Nothing got between the old man and his Sunday breakfast, not even this awkward discussion.

He watched his mother under-eye trying to read her face. She was chewing slowly, thoughtfully, and watching Zahara openly, as though reading her.

"You have," she said when she spoke again and there had been enough of a conversational lag that Zahara looked confused as to what she had done. "Been a good influence," his mother clarified.

Pappy burped then, and his mother broke her focus enough to snap at him, "Daddy!" His mother rolled her eyes in Zahara's direction as if to say, "Lord see mi crosses!"

Zahara giggled.

"Clearly he can't have too many good influences," his mother said.

And Pappy said, "What?" There was a twinkle in his grandfather's eye though that told him the belch was not entirely accidental. Maybe Pappy was not as oblivious to the weirdness as he appeared.

Zahara was laughing out loud by now, and he was beginning to relax a little bit, things were starting to feel more normal.

His mother's voice cut into the mellowness.

"Sometimes I worry, you know, with his daddy dying the way he did, being the way he was," she said. And she had everyone's attention at that. Even Pappy stopped eating. His mother never, ever talked about his father. "But he's not his daddy," she continued. She caught and held Zahara's eyes before saying more. "...any more than you're your mommy..."

Zahara's swallow was audible. He felt uncomfortable for both of them, but his mother still wasn't done.

"We all make ourselves. You hear what I'm saying?"

Her stern face softened. She even smiled a little when she said, "And what I see you making yourself into make me as a mother proud. I'm sure your granny must be proud too."

He looked from his mom's odd smile to Zahara's frozen face not sure what to do, or, for that matter, what to feel. He kind of wanted to comfort them both.

"Well"—and leave it to Pappy to once again try to break up the awkwardness—"the past is the past, eh," he said.

His mother's eyes went to his, and she held them, like she had stuff she wanted to say to him too. Shaka wasn't surprised. He figured she'd always known about Pappy going to Zahara's mother's funeral. Antigua was a small country. Pappy must have known that, too.

The old man didn't say anything. Just waited for her judgment, that's how it seemed to Shaka.

It worried him a little bit that the tight-tight family unit he'd always been able to count on might splinter, right there over Sunday breakfast, at the dining table they never used, in front of his girl. He wouldn't cry, he wouldn't cry.

"Yes," his mother said, "the past is the past." And his breath rushed out of him; that's when he realized he'd been holding it.

Zahara looked as shell-shocked as he felt.

Pappy and his mother weren't big on heart to hearts, though, so when his grandfather said "hm" and resumed eating, he could only assume that they had

260

finally put whatever unspoken misunderstandings lay between them to rest.

As for him, not only didn't he feel hungry anymore, he felt light headed, from the high of last night to whatever this was, he felt like he'd just stepped off of a particularly epic roller coaster.

Just then Zahara jumped up, the suddenness of it adding to his disorientation.

"Granny Linda go kill me," she said, rushing off to get her guitar, even as Pappy shouted after her, "Nuh worry 'bout that, me'll take you home."

Pappy got up, taking his plate with him, still eating, as he turned toward the kitchen.

He just sat there, not knowing what to do with himself, until his mother, with a gentle smile said, "you nar go tell your girl bye? Thought I raised you better than that."

He and Zahara waited for Pappy out by the car.

"She knows who I am," Zahara said.

"Yeah."

"That's not all she knows."

"Yeah."

By the time Pappy came out, keys jingling, they were laughing so hard, tears were streaming down both their faces.

Shaka was washing dishes while his mom cleared the table and packed away the leftovers when he blurted it out, between one of her short trips from kitchen to dining area and back again. He wasn't able to push the question down anymore.

"So you knew all the time?" he asked.

He didn't know whether she'd answer or not, which, to be honest, wasn't unusual; like most of his friends' mothers, she had selective hearing. And, in fact, he was putting the last glass on the rack when she spoke up.

"Yes, I figured it out," she said.

He turned. She was leaning against the counter, legs crossed at the ankle.

"She have her mother face, Zahara. But it really hit home *whanightee* when I meet her grandmother after you-all show. Can't hide. Plus, I know the mother face well. She was bare-faced, you see, didn't hide to do what she was doing, didn't care. But I just kept my head on and I was never one to fight another woman over a man. He knew what he was doing."

She sounded so sad. He wanted to hug her but didn't know how she'd receive it. They weren't a hugging family.

He'd always told himself he didn't feel anything about his father, but now anger sparked in him, burning out the only pleasant memory he had of the man. It was a vague memory of him on his father's back, hanging unto him as he swam through the water. There was a photograph of them together at the beach, him on his father's shoulders. He'd found it years ago, digging through his mother's things for something that at the time seemed important enough to risk the raasing he would get if he got caught going through his mother's things. That that photograph even existed made him doubt his own memory, like was it even a memory or something he'd made up in his mind to go with the picture, to fill a void. Looking at that picture had made him feel weird like it wasn't real, like the boy and man in it were figments of his imagination. But he told himself that it didn't matter because as far as he was concerned, his family was just this; Pappy, his mother, the Lion Crew, and now Zahara. That was much more than some people had, more he suspected than even his mother had. She had him and Pappy, but he knew she still mourned her own mother and had never really moved on from his father. Even now, even with her acceptance of Zahara, knowing the truth, the memory of his father still shadowed her eyes.

He gave in to instinct and took the two steps from the sink toward her. She tensed but he followed through with the motion anyway, hugged her, and held on when she would have pulled away, swatting at him, "boy!" He held on and after a time she relaxed into his embrace with a little shudder. He held on.

When he stepped back, her eyes were dry but red.

"You not your father," she said, and she tilted her chin up a little when she said it, like she was proud of having raised him to be different, better. Something burst open inside him, and he realized he'd needed to hear that, that when she looked at him she didn't see the man who had brought her pain.

"Zahara not her mother," she continued. "I not goin' judge her based on what her mother did. May her soul rest in peace."

His lips quirked at that. Pappy had said a similar thing when speaking of his father, as if despising the person in life was no reason to wish them ill in death.

She caught the quirk. "What?" she asked. "Laugh pon me?"

And grateful for the lifeline, he pretended to look her over, as though checking for the laugh—in her eyes, behind her neck, under her arm. He still had the reflexes to duck when she swatted her hand at him.

And the sound of her laugh when she did was the most beautiful sound.

Chapter

29

As promised, Pappy drove her home and he even came to the door and explained to Granny Linda that they'd invited her to have breakfast with them after church.

"Hope you don't mind, we just wanted to congratulate she and my grandson for doing so well."

She could only assume that Pappy's explanation took some of the heat out of what might otherwise have been waiting for her. She and Granny Linda might understand each other better now, but that didn't mean she could turn own-way by not coming straight home from church. Which is exactly what Granny Linda said to her after Pappy left. Her grandmother had also planned a special Sunday breakfast and now she

266

watched ruefully as Granny Linda put away the unused dishes.

"I'm sorry," she said. And she meant it too.

"I'm proud of you," Granny Linda replied, "but I not goin' put up with the wildness, no sneaking out, none of that. I goin' respect you but you must respect yourself too."

"Yes Granny, I'm sorry," she mumbled, contrite.

Granny Linda looked at her a moment longer as if searching for the lie then she nodded.

"And next time when I send you church, haul your tail straight home."

"Yes Granny."

Later, in her room, as she slipped into casual Sunday clothes, she realized that she'd been lucky; that there had definitely been a shift in things between her and Granny Linda. She wouldn't take it for granted.

She started to work on her paper, which reminded her... she picked up her cell and texted Nicola.

saw ur vid...cool.

In a minute, Nicola texted back.

Thx u were my inspiration.

She settled down to write her paper.

"I know this girl," she began and the character she described was a combination of girls like herself and

Joanne C. Hillhouse

Nicola, girls who instinctively learned to reject themselves even if no one outright told them to because everything from rap videos, to magazine covers, to the way people treated them told them they weren't beautiful. And not unlike in the "Brown Girl" poem, she imagined an ancestor visiting her character from the past and schooling her about her history, reminding her who she was, showing her the ways she rejected herself by rejecting others who looked just like her, all the while projecting a false sense of confidence.

She wrote about following the advice of Ms. George from the 'Brown Girl' video, how she'd sat in front of the mirror saying the words to "Phenomenal Woman" to herself, even putting them to music because she believed words mattered and music could change the world.

She wrote about bleaching, the damage it did to both the skin and the soul. She described it as a kind of body dysmorphia, a word she'd learned while watching a documentary about Michael Jackson after his death. It was a kind of mental illness, wanting to be something you'd never be, failing to recognize the wonderfulness that you already were.

"Slavery did a number on us," she wrote, "and now we continue to do it to ourselves because we don't see it for what it is. One of the cool things about doing this project is that I now see it. I see it in others and I see it in myself too. I see it not only in the ways I reject myself, but in the ways I respond to what's 'beautiful' and what's not. I didn't think I had those prejudices but I do; we all do, whether we know it or not. But now that I know better, hopefully I'll do better, think differently, and more fully embrace the beauty in all of us, whatever shade we come in."

She ended by quoting the lyrics to "Melanin." She planned to slip a CD of the song into the presentation folder, but for now she was just going to let the paper sit for a while, because her body was starting to crash, finally. Her bed was calling her, and not a moment too soon.

She discovered that the first day of school was no less nerve-wracking when you'd flowered over the summer.

As she walked into class, there was still that old familiar feeling of wanting to disappear into the floor as all around the room, her classmates loudly greeted each other and talked about their vacation. She wasn't allowed to though; a few of them had seen the play.

"You guys were so good," Chatty Cathy said.

"Yeah, and that Shaka boy who played Anansi, he can move," someone else, Wendy, said.

Both Cathy and Wendy were popular girls, the kind of girls who wouldn't normally notice her. She almost looked over her shoulder to see if they were talking to someone behind her…which was ridiculous because they were obviously talking about her.

"You know if he seeing anyone?" Kim asked.

"Who?"

"Anansi," the girl replied.

That took her by surprise. It made her realize that she'd gotten so used to everyone knowing that she and Shaka were an item.

"Yes," she said. "Me."

That shut them up. They studied her, not too subtly, as if trying to see what he saw in her. Once upon a time she might have wilted under that kind of scrutiny. She didn't now though and before they could say anything further, like maybe he wasn't all that cool after all, the teacher called them to order.

She was in a new form and had a new homeroom teacher, but the rest of the day's routine was familiar. When finally it was time for the Social Sciences class though, she looked up to see a strange man entering the room. He introduced himself as Mr. Otto. She felt her heart drop. Somehow, even with the personnel changes that sometimes happened from one year to the next, she hadn't anticipated the possibility that Mrs. Keener wouldn't be there.

She raised her hand. "Excuse me Mr. Otto. What about Mrs. Keener?" she asked stupidly, and some of the girls snickered.

"Was that your previous teacher?" He asked. "She's not coming back. Migrated, I think."

And though it made no sense, she felt betrayed, like Mrs. Keener had left her hanging.

"But I don't understand," she blurted out. She was disrupting the class now, she could tell by the frown on his face. "What about the project she gave us over the summer?"

Mr. Otto looked at her like she was slow and some of the girls, probably the ones who hadn't done the assignment, glared at her. There was more snickering and someone said, "shhhh." But she'd put a lot of work into that project over the summer and she couldn't believe that Mrs. Keener wouldn't be reading it. She'd imagined herself sitting with Mrs. Keener and talking with her about all she'd learned, and now she was just gone.

"I think it's safe to say you get a pass on that," Mr. Otto said, with a benign smile like he was doing them a favour. "Fresh start."

"But…" she started again.

"That's enough now," he interrupted. "Mrs. Keener isn't coming back and we're not looking back. Let's move on."

Zahara slouched in her chair, fuming, not really hearing anything he said after that.

That day, she ran into Nicola a few times in the tree-lined corridors. She'd had this little fear inside her that Nicola might ignore her once the summer was over, but she didn't. During break time, Nicola actually invited her to sit with her and some of her friends at the fifth form table under the flamboyant tree. She accepted. Nicola's friends had seen the play and were full of questions.

"I love that song, 'Melanin,'" one said. "You did that too, right?"

And somehow or the other, she found her tongue.

"Well, we all did," she responded. "Shaka and Ted and Nikki and me and the Crew."

"Shaka, he's the one that move like a snake," someone said.

"I think you mean a spider."

272

"No, a snake. Spiders are ewww."

Nicola caught her eye then and went cross-eyed, and she laughed.

After school she found Nicola waiting for her outside. Nicola offered her a ride, but she passed. She hadn't made any specific plans with Shaka, but she hoped he'd meet up with her on the way home so they could walk together like they used to when he was first trying to get with her.

He did. The Crew was there waiting for her too. So they walked and talked, filling each other in on their first day back. Shaka had been a minor celebrity at his school as well. The Crew had a grand time describing how they'd all been met like returning heroes. But Shaka, they said, had been treated like Bieber, Machel Montano, Tian Winter, or somebody.

"The ladies love Shaka Zulu," Kong joked. They all launched into the old LL Cool J rap, substituting Shaka's name. Except "LL Shaka Zulu" didn't quite have the same ring to it. Too many syllables or something.

After a while Shaka fell back and took her hand. She slowed her pace to match his and the boys made kissy sounds. Shaka rolled his eyes and shook his head, and she wasn't half as embarrassed as she once might have been. She and Shaka weren't doing anything more than holding hands—and occasionally kissing—and she was glad that it hadn't gone further than that; she wasn't ready for more. He hadn't said as much but he hadn't pushed her, so she figured he wasn't either.

"So you didn't get to turn in the project?" he said.

It made her feel like he got her that he picked up on her disappointment at that. She shook her head.

"Well, it's not like you didn't get anything out of doing it," he said, slinging an arm over her shoulder.

He was right of course. The truth was, doing that project had given her the summer of her life, and taught her some lessons she would never forget as long as she lived. So, yes, she'd gotten something out of it.

"Just not an 'A'," she grumped.

And Shaka smiled. "A much-deserved 'A'."

"A-plus," she pushed.

And he shook his head.

"Women. Always have to have the last word."

"You know it."

Just then, Kong shouted back. "Hey! walk up slowpokes, arwe waan stop for ice cream."

"I have to get home," she started to say.

"Ah aryuh ah keep arwe back, we coulda done reach by now. Pick up your feet."

They did just that. She was already thinking of her two scoops of chocolate and was secretly pleased that she was being treated like one of the boys. If it went on like this, she might even be performing with them at their next fête, an idea not as far-fetched as it might once have been.

CPSIA information can be obtained
at www.ICGtesting.com
Printed in the USA
LVHW010204050121
675671LV00004B/203